THE JUDAS FREAK

Also by Hugh Pentecost

Julian Quist Mystery Novels:
THE BEAUTIFUL DEAD
THE CHAMPAGNE KILLER
DON'T DROP DEAD TOMORROW

Pierre Chambrun Mystery Novels:
BARGAIN WITH DEATH
WALKING DEAD MAN
BIRTHDAY, DEATHDAY
THE DEADLY JOKE
GIRL WATCHER'S FUNERAL
THE GILDED NIGHTMARE
THE GOLDEN TRAP
THE EVIL MEN DO
THE SHAPE OF FEAR
THE CANNIBAL WHO OVERATE

John Jericho Mystery Novels:
A PLAGUE OF VIOLENCE
THE GIRL WITH SIX FINGERS
DEAD WOMAN OF THE YEAR
THE CREEPING HOURS
HIDE HER FROM EVERY EYE
SNIPER

The Judas Freak

HUGH PENTECOST

A RED BADGE NOVEL OF SUSPENSE

Dodd, Mead & Company · New York

Copyright © 1974 by Judson Philips
All rights reserved
No part of this book may be reproduced in any form
without permission in writing from the publisher

ISBN: 0-396-07001-9
Library of Congress Catalog Card Number: 74-10009
Printed in the United States of America
by The Haddon Craftsmen, Inc., Scranton, Penna.

Part One

ONE

Abigail Tyler was a good deal less sophisticated than you would have expected a twenty-two-year-old girl to be in that time and at that place. She had only been to New York a half a dozen times in her whole life. She'd been born and raised and still lived in the town of Dabney, Vermont. Nothing much ever happened in Dabney except an occasional blistering editorial by Walter Nichols—known as Old Nick locally—in the *Green Mountain Journal.* Abigail was a sometime reporter, sometime photographer, sometime cleaning woman, and sometime errand boy for the *Green Mountain Journal.* That explained why Abigail was in the Grand Ballroom of the Hotel Beaumont in New York City on that particular night. David Hale had been born in Dabney and this was David Hale's night of nights. Old Nick had thought the *Green Mountain Journal* should be represented, and there was no one to send but Abigail.

Abigail objected. She didn't have the clothes to wear at a ball. She would be tongue-tied if she had to talk to celebrities. She was secretly afraid that she might be confronted by someone she had dreamed of; someone like Steve McQueen, or Robert Redford, or Burt Reynolds. She had indulged in some fantasies about those glamorous gentlemen, and if she came face to face with one of them, she knew she would turn a bright, schoolgirl red and stammer like an idiot. She had spent some altogether too intimate times with them in her dreams. The party for David Hale was just the kind of affair any one of them might attend.

But Abigail went to the party in spite of her fears. Old Nick told her she had to, and her bread and butter depended on Old Nick. The only person she was commanded to interview was David Hale, the hometown boy who had made good in a big way. She was provided with a press pass, and a special dress for the occasion made by Miss Emily Whipple, Dabney's only dressmaker. The minute she appeared in it in the Grand Ballroom she wished she were dead. She had never seen so many beautiful and glamorous women in her lifetime, so many extravagant dresses, most of them revealing expanses of naked backs and fronts and even navels. Abigail felt like a mouse. She had never seen so much glittering jewelry. She had never seen so many handsome men, wearing a variety of evening clothes from the very mod to the traditional black-tie dinner jacket, almost all of them suntanned as if they'd spent their lives on tropical beaches. No sign of Burt Reynolds.

Not only the Beaumont's Grand Ballroom but some adjoining rooms were involved. There were three separate musical groups playing, a dozen or more bars in operation, overflowing buffets showing the most extraordinary-looking foods, prepared in the most extraordinary fashions Abigail had ever seen.

There was a little balcony above the ballroom and some of the press people had gathered there—people as glamorous and sophisticated as the guests. There was no chance in the early stages to get to David Hale, dark and mysterious looking—like a modern Heathcliff, Abigail thought. Hale and his wife, Peggy, were still part of a sort of reception line. Everyone embraced, everyone called everyone else "darling" and rushed for the nearest bar.

Abigail would have felt very lost, might have followed her impulse to run, if it hadn't been for a very nice young man whose job it was to see that "the press" were happy. He introduced himself as Bobby Hilliard and he looked and sounded a little like the young Jimmy Stewart Abigail had seen on the late, late movies on TV in Dabney.

Abigail was sitting down at the front of the little balcony looking down at the sea of glamour when she noticed two new arrivals, a man and a woman.

"Who are *they*?" Abigail asked Bobby Hilliard.

"She may be the most beautiful woman in the world," Bobby Hilliard said. "She is probably the most beautiful woman in America, and certainly the most beautiful one here tonight. Her name is—"

"The *man!*" Abigail said. The man was tall, blond, slim, wearing a pink dinner jacket. Blond wasn't the proper word to describe his golden hair. It was worn modishly long, and Abigail was reminded of the exquisite face on an old Greek coin. The dark girl, whose arm was slipped through the man's, was certainly an eyeful, but the *man!*

"That's Julian Quist," Bobby Hilliard said. "He's my boss. And the girl is Lydia Morton, who also works for him—and is his girl, in case anyone has ideas about either one of them."

"Wow!" Abigail said.

Bobby Hilliard grinned at her. "Care to meet them?"

"*Meet* them!"

"Sure. I have to report to Julian anyway. Come along."

"Oh, I *couldn't!*" Abigail said, and almost ran to keep up with Bobby as he headed down the main staircase to the ballroom floor. Burt Reynolds, for the moment, was forgotten.

The stairway from the balcony led down into what was a very large coat room, with a dozen pretty hat check girls on duty. Men and women, still arriving for David Hale's party, were checking coats and wraps. Men, their things already checked, were milling around, waiting for ladies who had gone to the powder room. Over the buzz of conversation and the soft music from Eddie Eager's band in the main ballroom, Abigail heard a high shrill voice, almost screaming.

"You sonofabitch!"

As if they had been ballet drilled, people backed off to make a sort of circle. A man who had just put his coat down for one of the hat check girls turned so that he was facing Abigail's way, where she stood, suddenly clinging to Bobby Hilliard's arm. He was a solidly built man, probably not yet forty, Abigail thought. His hair was dark, worn long. His eyebrows were coal black, as was a thin Fu Manchu mustache over a very white, very bright smile.

Facing this man was a small man, with sandy disheveled hair and wire-rimmed glasses. This was the name caller, and he took a wild swing at the dark man. It was a bad scene. The dark man parried the little man's punch, he swung sidearm and knocked the little man to his knees and sent the wire-rimmed glasses skidding across the floor. Then, as the little man tried to rise, the dark man chopped at him with a savage, karate-type blow to the side of his neck. The little man was down—and very still. The dark man stepped forward and lifted his foot, with the obvious intention of stomping on the little man's face.

Abigail screamed, wondering why no one interfered. And then someone did. A man, who for a moment Abigail thought was Joe Mannix out of television, pushed the dark man off balance. This man, who, after all, wasn't Joe Mannix, hunched his shoulders inside a well-tailored black dinner jacket.

"You want a workout, Max-baby, I'll be happy to oblige," he said.

Max-baby raised a hand to suck at a bruised knuckle. "I rarely take on professionals, Dan," he said.

"Or anyone who can fight back," the man who wasn't Joe

Mannix said. He looked around the circle of faces. "Let's not spoil David's party," he said. "If Mr. Robson wants a little extra exercise, I'll be available." He bent down and helped the little man to his feet.

"My glasses!" the little man muttered.

Somebody produced them. Max Robson continued to suck a knuckle. "I didn't start this, as plenty of witnesses can testify," he said.

"I'd guess nothing happens to you that you don't start, Max," a cool voice said from behind Abigail. She turned and found herself looking up at the golden man in the pink jacket with the luscious dark girl still attached to his arm.

"Julian, Dan and I will take care of Terry Smallwood," Bobby Hilliard said, "if you'll take care of Miss Abigail Tyler. Abigail represents the *Green Mountain Journal,* which is the newspaper in David's hometown."

Julian Quist looked down at Abigail and she felt her knees turning to water. He was the most fabulous-looking man she had ever seen. He was just plain beautiful, if you could say that about a man.

"Our fight scenes are usually staged in Madison Square Garden, Abbie," he said, smiling. "I could stand a drink if you could. By the way, this is Lydia Morton."

Lydia Morton smiled cheerfully at Abigail, who felt mousier than ever contrasting herself to the dark girl.

"Ten to one nobody calls Miss Tyler 'Abbie,' Julian," Lydia said. "She's far too attractive to be an Abbie. It's Gail, isn't it, Miss Tyler?"

Abigail was close to swooning. Of course, everyone in Dabney called her Abbie. In her fantasies her dream men had called her Gail. Nobody could think of romance with a girl named Abbie. How had Lydia Morton known?

Bobby Hilliard and the man called Dan were taking the little victim of the fight into the men's room. Abigail, not really believing it, found herself walking between Quist and Lydia, each with a hand on an arm, being guided to a table at the far end of the ballroom. Unbelievably, she found herself sitting next to Quist, found a glass of sparkling Burgundy in her hands, knew herself surrounded by jewels and perfume and the tempting music of Eddie Eager's boys.

"Somebody really ought to do something about Max Robson," Lydia said.

"Was that—was that Max Robson, the famous critic?" Abigail asked.

"The word infamous might be more appropriate—Gail," Quist said.

He had called her Gail! It sounded just as she had imagined it would sound, coming from a romantic man. Somebody touched her shoulder and she found Bobby Hilliard there.

"Terry lost a tooth in addition to his dignity," he said. "We put him in a cab and sent him home." He smiled at Abigail. "Don't you think we should try the music?"

And so the magic world of the famous, and the rich, and the very important enveloped Abigail Tyler of Dabney, Vermont. She found herself dancing with Bobby Hilliard, who was unexpectedly conservative, and with the man who wasn't Joe Mannix and who turned out to be Dan Garvey and who was nothing short of fantastic on the dance floor, and finally she was floating in the arms of the unbelievable Julian Quist when—her dress strap broke. Overcome by confusion lest she should suddenly become exposed on the dance floor, she stammered an excuse and bolted for the powder room.

It had been a big night for David Hale—a coming into national stardom at age thirty-eight. He had been launched on this night as the host on a late-night television talk show, bucking the world of Johnny Carson. "Night Talk," the show was called, and a long-term contract with the network guaranteed that he'd be talking to all the famous, glamorous, and exciting people in the world five days a week for at least the next five years. It meant money in unbelievable amounts for David and for the people he had gathered together as his staff. It meant a kind of power which he knew, on this first night, he would never abuse.

The whole amazing success had come at just the right time in his life. He had married a very nice, straightforward, simple girl who was in his class in college. They were both twenty. David, who at that time was young enough and handsome enough to have played Heathcliff for Miss Abigail Tyler—who was then only four years old—was going to be an actor. Peggy was going to be a wife and write the great American novel on the side. They were very much in love. They took off for Hollywood, because Broadway was sick and the only action for a hopeful actor was in television. Television was almost entirely in Hollywood. David got a few small bits to play and then, fortunately for the family exchequer, some commercials. Peggy made all the difficulties seem worthwhile. Sooner or later, he knew, he would make it in a big way. He would be a new Robert Redford, a new Sean Connery. It seemed like a long time in coming until the day he got a small part in a new Janice Trail film. Janice Trail was Hollywood's newest sex symbol. Even though his part was small David knew that everyone in the world would see him. His moment in front of the camera involved a very intimate, very sexy scene with the star. Peggy kidded him about it. How could she possibly compete with Janice Trail?

The unfortunate answer was that she couldn't. Miss Trail's sexuality was not some kind of studio buildup. The minute she and David began to rehearse their scene, the minute they touched each other, David was lost, dazzled, gone. Miss Trail seemed equally lost, dazzled, and gone. There was no way to have a private affair with Janice Trail. She wore her lovers like jewels in public. David was suddenly her number one boy. David tried for a while to battle it, like a hooked alcoholic. He loved Peggy, but Janice was a drug he couldn't resist. So after a while Peggy gave him his freedom by way of a divorce, and David slept between silken sheets with America's sex queen for all the world to see and envy.

Being Janice Trail's lover did not, however, advance his acting career. What did his acting career matter, Janice asked him? He should just eat lots of protein, take lots of vitamins, and be ready to take care of Janice's erotic needs whenever she asked for it, which was actually oftener than any one man could satisfy. And David didn't like being doled out an allowance like a gigolo. So he worked wherever he could find it, no matter how unimportant. He was offered a chance to narrate a documentary which nobody would probably ever look at. He was handsome and he had a good voice and speech. Maybe the public didn't flock to see the documentary, but the head of a local television station did. He wanted a newscaster who would be attractive enough to buck the competition of Walter Cronkite and John Chancellor. It was acting, in a sense. A staff provided David with his script. He just had to read it impressively.

Somehow he caught on in the world of news. The scriptwriter on his show had very little humor, and David took to ad-libbing a few quips of his own. It went very well, and he became a kind of local celebrity. Someone from the network saw the show and began to turn some wheels. When David was offered a job on the network staff in New York he took it. His working hours had interfered with Janice Trail's appetite and he was aware that other people were operating between those silk sheets.

And so, after two years of being the luscious lady's number one stud, he took off for New York, feeling somehow free and yet a little lost. He began to make his mark as a newscaster and commentator, supervising his own material. He was on some of the panel shows. He asked some pretty disturbing questions during the Senate Watergate hearings. He was not the kind of actor he had intended to be but he was, nonetheless, an actor. That fact contributed to his success.

One day, when he was lunching at a posh little French restaurant west of Broadway, he saw Peggy. He looked at her and he knew what had caused the hollow feeling in the pit of his stomach for so long. He was hungry for her, he loved her.

He walked over to Peggy's table and sat down facing her. Neither one of them spoke for a long time, and then David, smiling that crooked little smile of his that charmed millions of viewers every day, said: "I hope you won't think I'm rushing things, lady, but will you marry me sometime later today?"

"Is marriage essential?" she asked.

"With you—yes," he said. "I've discovered that there isn't any kind of life without you, so I want it total. We could drive out to wherever one drives out to, and be married before supper."

"I do," Peggy said.

"You will?"

"I do—promise to love, honor and obey, till death do us part," Peggy said. "And it will be death that parts us, David. If you run out on me again I will slit your handsome throat."

"And I will provide the slitter. Is it too sensational, do you think, to kiss a lady in a French restaurant?"

And so they were married again, and lived happily ever after—or at least until that night in the Beaumont ballroom.

*   *   *

Inventing images was Julian Quist's profession. The offices of Julian Quist Associates were in a glass and steel finger that pointed to the sky over Grand Central Station. The offices were as "mod" as Quist's pink dinner jacket, the colors were pale pastels, the walls decorated with paintings, changed fairly frequently, by modern artists who were very much "with it." Modern furniture promised discomfort and turned out to be unexpectedly relaxing. The reception room was presided over by the glamorous Miss Gloria Chard, wearing her simple little Rudi Gernreich creations, looking as if she had been put together by some genius in the art of female allure.

Among the primary people who made Julian Quist Associates work, after the man himself, was Lydia Morton, looking more like a high fashion model than the brilliant researcher and writer she was. Lydia kept an elaborate wardrobe in Quist's Beekman Place apartment and rarely slept in her own apartment in her own bed which was a couple of blocks away. Dark, handsome Dan Garvey was another, a former professional football player, who kept a Phi Beta Kappa key hidden away, for fear, Quist had said, someone might discover he had a brain as well as a body. Bobby Hilliard was another, looking, as Abigail Tyler had thought, like a young Jimmy Stewart, a genius at handling people who needed persuasion with an apparently unsophisticated tact. And a key cog in the machine was Quist's private secretary, Constance Parmalee, red-haired, with beautiful legs that would always keep the mini-skirt popular, wide greenish gray eyes that were partly concealed by tinted granny glasses, and a secret she thought she kept and which everyone knew. Her secret was that she wished she could trade places with Lydia Morton.

Several months before David Hale's opening night party Quist found himself approached by Michael Grant, president of the International Television Network—ITN. Michael Grant was Madison Avenue, from the top of his carefully styled hairdo to the toes of his highly polished custom-made shoes. Quist had been involved in more than one business deal with Micky Grant, and there was a note stashed away in his mental computer to beware of Cheryl Grant, Micky's wife, who was a manhunter armed with razor blades.

Micky unfolded the network's plans for David Hale. A show called Night Talk, to be thrown into direct competition with Johnny Carson.

"Not an experiment," Micky said. "Betz and Smallwood have got us a client who will sponsor Hale for five years, win, lose or draw—with one loophole only. Morals."

"From what I know of David you're home free," Quist said. He was sitting behind his very mod desk in his very mod office, smoking a long, thin cigar.

"There was Janice Trail," Micky said.

"What more could Middle America ask for?" Quist asked. "Our hero marries a lovely girl, is swept off his feet by a sinister Delilah, sees the error of his ways and remarries the original lovely girl. The prodigal, expiating his sins."

"You sound very biblical this morning, Julian."

"You mentioned morals," Quist said.

"You don't think David might run off with some other glamour puss?"

" 'Who knows what evil lurks in the hearts of men?' " Quist quoted from an old radio drama. "Seriously, I can't answer for what happens to any man who gets backed into a corner by a wide-open doll. My guess is David has had his runaway period."

"Would you undertake a campaign for David?"

Quist grinned at Micky. "I wondered how long you'd have the nerve to keep asking for free advice, chum," he said.

*   *   *

In three months of working to get the image of David Hale into the public eye Quist had come to know the man and his wife quite well. David's charm was not a veneer; he was wise, and witty, and shrewd in his observations and evaluations. David and Peggy had dined with Quist and Lydia several times; it got friendly and quite casual—cocktail hours, long bull sessions on the terrace of Quist's apartment, a couple of home-cooked spaghetti dinners prepared by Peggy. Peggy, an elfin quality to her freckled Irish face, was very special, Quist thought. She knew her man and she loved him. She'd regaled them with the story of how they'd remarried the first time they'd seen each other after their divorce.

"If more women could really forgive," Lydia said later, "there would be a great many more happy women."

"Men are such beasts," Quist said. They were lying together in the king-sized bed in his apartment and he was holding her very close. There was nothing quite so delightful as having conversation when your hands caressed.

"Women are not different from men, Julian," Lydia said. "We have a problem though. You can attack; we have to wait to be attacked."

Quist laughed. "Who is the aggressor?" he asked. "The animal who goes after the meat in the trap, or the trapper? It amuses me to think that you constantly attack me, luv."

"It really doesn't matter, does it, as long as we both want the same outcome?" And Lydia kissed him gently and very tenderly.

And then, after three months of hard work, David Hale was launched. Guests gathered in the ballroom at the Beaumont, they watched his first show on a dozen monitors, and then after the show was over—at about one-thirty in the morning, actually—David and Peggy arrived at the party and it was launched full-blown.

"It would seem you've been deserted, master," Lydia said

to Quist. Miss Abigail Tyler had left him on the dance floor and rushed in a disorderly retreat to the powder room. Half an hour had passed and she hadn't come back.

"Poor kid, her dress started to fall off," Quist said. "She probably hasn't been able to find a needle and thread."

"At the Beaumont?" Dan Garvey said. "There are people waiting in the wings with needles and threads. And anything else you might dream of." And then he made a kind of growling noise. "Can you beat that for gall?"

Quist followed his gaze out to the center of the dance floor.

"What a bitch," Lydia said. "Couldn't she have let him alone?"

Dancing happily in the arms of Max Robson was Miss Janice Trail, America's sex queen, the "other woman" in David Hale's life. She hadn't been invited to the party, that was certain. But who could turn away such a famous lady from any party? Quist thought of cutting in and telling the lady what he thought of her, but just as he was rising from his chair Micky Grant, the head of the International Television Network, grabbed his arm with fingers that bit hard.

"I've got to talk to you, Julian—in private!" Micky's face looked pale under his sunlamp tan.

"What's wrong?"

"Now—in private, Julian!"

Quist nodded and turned to Lydia. "Be a nice girl, will you, luv, and see what's happened to our Miss Tyler? She may need help." He smiled. "Tell her not to worry, I didn't see anything I shouldn't have."

He walked with Micky Grant out of the ballroom and into the Beaumont's lobby. Micky took an envelope out of his pocket and handed it to Quist. It was a plain envelope, unmarked, Micky's name and nothing else typed on it. Quist opened it and took out a plain sheet of paper. As he did something fell out of the paper onto the floor. It was, he saw, a small snapshot. Micky Grant bent down to pick it up while Quist read the three typewritten lines on the piece of paper.

> If you want to avert a total disaster investigate the story the enclosed snapshot will lead you to. I will never let you get away with promoting David Hale.

Quist took the snapshot from Micky Grant's unsteady fingers. It was a picture of a man in a business suit, wearing black glasses. It was impossible to get a clear look at his face because it was partly turned away and looking down at a small boy—ten or twelve years old, Quist guessed. Quist couldn't remember that he had ever seen the man or the boy. The man certainly wasn't David, and the boy was not David twenty-five years ago. David was dark, and the boy in the snapshot was almost albino blond.

"Some kind of crackpot," Quist said, just to say something. He was disturbed. "How did it come to you? When?"

"Fifteen, twenty minutes ago. A hotel bellhop. He said it was delivered by a messenger service. One for me, one for Jake Betz of Betz and Smallwood, the ad agency, and one for Gerald Laverick of Laverick Enterprises, the sponsor."

"You compared notes?"

"Not yet. They don't know from me that I know they've got one of these. But there is going to be all hell to pay, Julian."

It crossed Quist's mind that earlier in the evening Terry Smallwood, of Betz and Smallwood, had taken a poke at Max Robson, the television critic. He wondered if there was any connection.

"There doesn't seem much else to do but talk to David," he said.

TWO

Quist knew the night house manager of the Beaumont from having worked with him to arrange this evening. Was there an office or a private room somewhere on this floor where Quist could hold a brief conference with some friends? There was, directly behind the front desk. The night bell captain was dispatched with a message to David Hale, asking the star of the evening to join Quist there for a few moments.

Quist and Micky Grant went to the little back office to wait. Grant was giving a very fair imitation of Mr. Coffee Nerves.

"There are literally millions of dollars involved here, Julian," Grant said. "David's salary for five years, salaries to his staff, the producer, the director. There's the cost of network time and all the people working that side of the street. Commissions to Betz and Smallwood on millions in advertising, chiefly from Laverick Enterprises but including a dozen other smaller buyers of time. It's disasterville if that goddamn letter is for real."

Quist had perched himself on the edge of a shiny-topped stretcher table. He was frowning through the smoke from one of his long, thin cigars at the snapshot of the man with the black glasses and the blond boy.

"I'm no photography buff," he said, ignoring Grant's litany of despair, "but there are some interesting things about this picture. If you'll look at it closely, Micky, you'll see that it has a kind of faded look to it, suggesting it was taken a long time ago. But the paper on which it's printed is quite fresh and new. A today copy of a yesterday picture."

"So?"

"So whatever this is supposed to suggest is something from some time ago—quite a long time ago, I'd say."

"David will be able to tell us," Grant said.

"I hope," Quist said.

And then David came, his handsome face dark with anger.

"Don't ask me, let me tell you," he said. "I didn't ask Janice Trail to come here tonight. It's just a sample of her bitchy way to make the evening less than charming for me, to take something away from it for Peggy."

"I wouldn't even have bothered to ask you," Quist said. "It's something else, David." He handed the snapshot and the threatening note to his friend.

David scowled, first at the photograph and then at the note. "What in Christ's name—," he said.

"Mean something to you?" Quist asked.

"But nothing!" David said, still studying the note and the snapshot.

"Micky thinks duplicates of this have been sent to Jake Betz and Gerald Laverick," Quist said.

"And God knows who else!" Grant said.

"You don't know the people in the picture?" Quist asked.

David drew a deep breath. "Never saw them before in my life," he said. He looked up and handed the things back to Quist.

Quist felt a kind of cold anger settle over him. He had an instinct for truth. Just as sure as God David was lying.

"I'm going to tell Laverick and Betz it's nothing," Grant said. "Some kind of crackpot nonsense."

"You do that," Quist said.

Quist flicked the ash from his cigar into a brass dish on the table as Grant left him alone with David.

"I'm as safe as your priest or your psychiatrist, David," he said.

"I don't follow."

"If it's nothing so what's to worry? If it's something there has to be a way to fight it."

"I tell you, Julian, it doesn't mean anything to me," David said.

"Have it your way," Quist said, his voice cold.

For just a moment Quist thought David was going to tell him something, but the moment passed.

"I'd better get back to Peg," David said. He smiled. "I don't ordinarily like big parties, but this is a great one, Julian. Thanks."

"You only hit the jackpot once in this business," Quist said. "If you change your mind about telling me, chum, I won't hold it against you that you delayed—unless you delay too long."

"I swear to you, Julian—"

"Don't!" Quist said, sharply. "I might ask you to swear to something some other time. I'd want to believe you when that time comes—if it comes."

Back in the ballroom Quist found his table deserted. Lydia was dancing with an actor-client of the office; Bobby Hilliard was back in the press balcony; and Dan Garvey was standing at one of the bars across the way, talking to dark, heavy-set Jake Betz of the advertising agency. Quist beckoned to a waiter. He wanted something a little more medicinal to drink than sparkling Burgundy. A double Jack Daniels on the rocks was what the doctor ordered.

Lydia spotted her man, and she and her dance partner came over to the table. There were polite greetings from the actor.

"I'm afraid your little girl friend turned out to be Abbie

after all," Lydia said. "She seems to have flown the coop. She didn't even ask the attendant in the powder room for a needle and thread, which was, of course, available."

"Odd she'd go without doing her job," Quist said. "She was supposed to interview David, I understand."

"Panic," Lydia said.

"One broken dress strap?"

"In Dabney, Vermont, that's probably a social disaster," Lydia said. She hesitated. She knew her man. The set of his mouth, the cold distant look in his eyes warned her that something was wrong. "You want me to follow up on the girl, Julian?"

"Not just now, luv," Quist said. "Later I may need to find her."

He saw Micky Grant bearing down on the table and he waved Lydia and her partner back to the dance floor. Grant looked white and worried.

"Laverick and Betz got duplicates of my note," he said.

"Pictures too?"

Grant nodded. "I told them the picture meant nothing to David. I'm not sure either of them bought it. Laverick insists on a conference in his office tomorrow morning at ten. Betz and David and I are ordered to attend. Your presence is requested. Laverick is afraid we may need your help."

"With what?"

"Whatever kind of trouble we're in," Grant said. "You will come, won't you, Julian?"

"Nobody's going to leave this party till breakfast," Quist said. "Isn't ten o'clock a little early?"

"Not with umpteen million bucks at stake," Grant said. "Not with Gerald Laverick at the controls. He's already gone home to be ready."

Quist stared out at the dance floor where Janice Trail, the golden girl of sex, was the center of attention, being cut in on by a horde of gentlemen who appeared to be coming through a revolving door.

"Do you know what Terry Smallwood's brawl with Max Robson was all about?" he asked.

"That bastard!" Grant said. "Somebody on a morning paper read Terry Max's review to tonight's show."

"Unfavorable, of course?"

"Of course. Max is only happy when he destroys. But what blew Terry was his friend told him Max had handed in his review two days ago. He didn't—and I quote—'need to see the show to know how bad David Hale would be.'"

"Someday Max will accidentally cut his own throat," Quist said.

"Or inspire some hero to do it for him. You will come to Laverick's office in the morning?"

"If I'm awake," Quist said.

"We need someone there who won't be hysterical," Grant pleaded. "Knowing you, I know Laverick won't scare you."

"Nobody scares me, Micky, because nobody owns any part of me. Unless—" and Quist smiled—"unless it's Lydia, who owns all of me if she wants to claim it."

"Lucky you. Lucky her," Grant said. "You believe David, don't you?"

Quist looked out at the dance floor again where he spotted David dancing with his wife. "I trust him," he said, avoiding a literal answer.

A man whose business is building public images knows that there are always two sides to every coin. There is a side you embellish and exploit, and there is a side you try to keep turned away from public view. The bad side is not necessarily 'bad' in a moral or a legal sense. A man may perform a heroic act and be basically a coward. He may give a generous gift and be basically a miser. He may appear to be a happy family man and keep a chick down some back street for reasons a sympathetic friend might understand. In the three months Quist had gotten to know David Hale well while he was building a public image of the man, he had concluded that there was very little on the other side of the coin that needed to be hidden. There was the breakup of his marriage and the affair with Janice Trail, of course, but there was no way to hide that. The public would forgive that adventure because David had gone back to his wife, his first love. He was highly professional at his job. He never played the 'star' with people who worked with him. He was patient, untemperamental, and generous with his time and help if someone had a trouble. Quist believed he definitely belonged in the camp of the "good guys." Now there was a picture of a tall man wearing black glasses and a small blond boy—and a threat.

The actor-client brought Lydia back to the table.

"I think I'd like to go home," Quist said.

Lydia smiled at him. "I thought you'd never ask," she said. "I really loathe big parties. I've had three invitations to look at etchings, but I rather counted on you."

"I only make love to you because I need your talents at the office," Quist said.

"I only make love to you because I need the job," Lydia said.

They got up from the table and headed for the coat room. Quist caught Bobby Hilliard's eye and signaled to him to join them. While one of the hat check girls was finding Lydia's things, Quist took Bobby aside.

"You happen to know where that Green Mountain girl is staying?" Quist asked.

"Lord, no. I mean I had no reason to ask for her address, Julian. Not that one!"

"She skipped after she thought I'd had a peek at her bosom," Quist said. "She must have come loaded with a lot of hometown facts about David. For a special reason I wanted to pump her for them."

Bobby grinned. "You've got easy access to all the facts about David, boss. Lydia did the research on him for the campaign. Had you forgotten?"

"No, but I was interested in the local viewpoint," Quist said.

"What's to worry?" Bobby asked. "You've launched him like a moon rocket. Our job's done."

"I hope," Quist said.

In a taxi Quist and Lydia sat close together. "Something's bothering you," she said. "Naturally I'm dying of curiosity, but don't tell me if you don't want to."

He told her.

"And David says he doesn't know or recognize the picture?"

"He was lying," Quist said.

"How do you know?"

"Instinct."

"I covered every step of the way on David," Lydia said. "There wasn't even any smoke anywhere, let alone fire. I've researched a lot of people, Julian, and this man is about as clean as anyone I ever worked on. Except for the Janice Trail business, which is public history, there is nothing!"

"He refused to help an old lady cross the street when he was a boy scout?"

"Nothing."

"This snapshot could be twenty, twenty-five years old," Quist said. "Fresh copy of a snapshot that old. He would have been a boy scout about then."

"The Halstrohms were a respected, hard-working family," Lydia said.

"Halstrohms?"

"That was the family name, Julian. David changed it to Hale when he went into acting as a career. Nothing unusual about that. His father worked for the Vermont Marble Company. The father and mother were killed in a railroad crossing accident in nineteen fifty. David was fourteen. He was left pretty well off. His father's lawyer, a Dabney man, brought him up after that. He went to a local high school and then to Middlebury. Peggy, too. They were married during their senior year at college. David was popular—well liked, as Willy Loman would say. Not a breath of scandal anywhere, not even any bad mouthing by anyone."

The taxi pulled up outside the apartment building on Beekman Place. The night man in the lobby handed Quist an envelope.

"Messenger left this for you sometime around one o'clock, Mr. Quist."

It was the same kind of envelope as one Quist had been shown earlier by Micky Grant, plain, his name typed on it. He opened it and this time he didn't drop the snapshot it contained.

> You must be dying to solve the mystery, Mr. Quist.
> The snapshot is really your first clue. It could be called the long and the short of it.

It was the same snapshot of the man wearing black glasses and the blond boy. Quist handed it to Lydia and they headed for the elevator. They didn't speak until they were alone in his apartment.

"Make anything of it?" he asked.

Her bare shoulders moved in a little shudder. "Anonymous letters and threats give me the willies," she said.

"The snapshot isn't of anyone you came across in your research?"

"No."

*   *   *

It seemed like a long time later that Quist woke up, aware that the red button on the bedside phone was flashing on and off. There was no bell on that instrument. He had drawn the drapes over the windows to shut out imminent daylight. His first impulse was to reach out for Lydia to make sure that she was there and safe. She made a loving sound in her sleep as he touched her.

Then he picked up the phone.

"Julian? I'm sorry to call you when I know you must be asleep. But I've got trouble."

It was David Hale, and his voice sounded shaken.

"What is it, David?"

"Peggy and I just got home," David said. "There—there's a dead girl in our apartment."

Quist sat up so abruptly that it woke Lydia. "A dead girl!"

"She appears to have been shot, Julian."

"You've called the police?"

"No."

"Why not?"

"I wanted—to get your advice."

"Do you know who the girl is?"

"Yes."

"Well, for Christ sake, who is she?" Quist almost shouted.

"She's a kid from my home town. Dabney. She works—worked—on the paper there. Her name is Tyler."

"Abigail Tyler?"

"You know her?"

"Oh, God," Quist said.

"She was supposed to do an interview with me," David said. "Peggy and I asked her to have breakfast with us after the party. Special treatment for a hometown girl. I knew we'd have to stay at the Beaumont to the bitter end, so I told her if she got tired of the party she could come on ahead of us. I gave her Peg's key. And—and here she is."

"The doorman see her come? Was there anyone with her?"

"I haven't asked him. Peggy thought we should ask you—what to do."

"Jesus, man!"

"Well, what do we do, Julian?"

"You sit very tight," Quist said. "I'm going to try to reach a friend of mine. He's in Homicide—a Lieutenant Kreevich. Pray that I get him, because you've got to call the police. If I find Kreevich, there'll be a patrol car there before I can get there. Tell them a straight story, David."

"Yes."

"Does Abigail Tyler relate in any way to that snapshot?"

"Julian, I told you—"

"I know what you told me! When I get there you're really going to have to tell me. Don't lie to the police. Don't lie to Kreevich if he gets there ahead of me. If Abigail has no connection with that snapshot or the letters, don't mention them until we've had a chance to talk. But if she does—"

"I swear to God there is no connection, Julian. I don't know this girl. I met her at the studio last night just before the show went on. She had a letter from Walter Nichols, who edits the local paper and whom I've known all my life. As a favor to him, really, Peggy and I invited her to breakfast."

"So sit tight. When the cops come keep your cool."

"We'll try. And thanks."

THREE

Lydia had slipped out of bed while Quist talked with David.

"I'll have coffee for you when you're dressed," she said. It was typical of her that she didn't waste time with questions. Quist was grateful not to have to talk for a few minutes because he found himself in the grip of a kind of cold fury. Violence was not a new experience for him. His life and his business were enmeshed with high-powered people in high-powered situations and he found himself confronted from time to time with jarring explosions. But Abigail Tyler! She had been such a child, such a wide-eyed innocent.

Quist pulled the curtains in his dressing room and saw that it was already a bright, sunny morning. Seven-thirty, his watch told him. David and Peggy had stayed at the Beaumont to the bitter end if David had called as soon as they got home and found the girl.

Quist looked up Lieutenant Mark Kreevich's number in an address book and found himself in luck when he dialed. Kreevich answered after the first ring.

"What are you doing up so early in the morning?" Kreevich asked, cheerfully. "I figured you and your lady would 'have danced all night.' "

"Trouble," Quist said. "David Hale and his wife just got home."

"I watched the show," Kreevich said. "He was good, no

matter what Max Robson had to say on the subject. What's the trouble?"

"David found a girl shot to death in his apartment when he got home," Quist said.

"Has he called the police?" Kreevich asked, his voice suddenly crisp and professional.

"He's calling them now by way of me."

"Address?"

Quist gave the address on East Sixty-third Street.

"Does he know who the girl is?"

"From his hometown—reporter for the local newspaper," Quist said. "Her name is Abigail Tyler."

"She staying with the Hales?"

"She was invited for breakfast. David had given her a key in case they were held up at the party."

"You want in?" Kreevich asked.

"He's my friend as well as a client," Quist said.

"See you there," Kreevich said, and hung up.

The Hales had rented their East Side apartment when they'd remarried. It was a duplex in what was an elaborately remodeled old private home. Their living room was on the ground floor with a little garden at the back. Not too hard for a break in, Quist thought, if someone had it in mind. It occurred to him, as he slipped into a dark gray wool jacket, that there might be no connection at all between David's problems and the shooting of Abigail. Anyone at all interested would have known that the Hales would be at the Beaumont most of the night. It would have been an ideal time for a thief to have entered the apartment for the simple purpose of a robbery. Abigail, arriving much earlier than a thief could have expected, might have caught him redhanded and he had shot her.

"I hope to God it's that," Quist said to Lydia, grateful for the coffee she had waiting for him.

"But you don't think it is?"

"I have a feeling this isn't David's lucky day."

"What can I do?" Lydia asked.

"Abigail worked for the paper in Dabney," Quist said. "The editor is someone named Walter Nichols. David knows him well, apparently. Try to get Nichols on the phone, tell him what's happened, and find out about the girl's family and the best way to notify them. I may call you to find out when I get to David's."

Ten minutes later Quist was getting out of a taxi in front of the Sixty-Third Street house. There were two police cars parked in front. Quist walked into the small lobby where a frightened doorman was being questioned by a team of uniformed cops. He gave his name and said that Lieutenant Kreevich was expecting him. Kreevich had left word, and Quist rang the Hales' doorbell. At the same moment half a dozen men came in from the street. Quist recognized them as Kreevich's crew from Homicide and probably an assistant medical examiner.

A uniformed cop opened the apartment door and Quist slipped in ahead of the others. He knew the apartment well. Peggy had cooked two spaghetti dinners for him and Lydia here. There was a living room, a fairly good-sized kitchen, and a bath on this floor, and two bedrooms and a bath upstairs. French doors opened out into the garden.

Mark Kreevich, a short, square man with a boyish face and an intense manner, was talking with David at the far end of the room, notebook in hand. In the center of the floor Abigail's body was covered with a sheet. Peggy Hale, when she saw Quist, came running to him and literally threw herself into his arms.

"Oh, my God, Julian! Oh, my God!" she whispered, struggling with convulsive sobs.

Kreevich broke away from David when he saw his men

crowding in from the lobby.

"There's an upstairs?" he asked.

Quist nodded.

"You and Mr. and Mrs. Hale might better wait up there," the detective said. "There are routines."

Quist put his arm around Peggy and led her to the stairway. David, looking like a man in a trance, followed behind them. The first bedroom was as large as the living room, sunny and bright on this morning. It was half bedroom, half sitting room. A desk, a love seat, a couple of comfortable wing chairs near the windows; a large, happy-looking double bed at the far end. Closets with sliding doors revealed elaborate collections of male and female clothes. It was a room that looked lived in and loved in.

Peggy went to the windows, fighting to get control of herself. David stood beside Quist, not able to accomplish the business of lighting a cigarette.

"Thanks for coming," he said. "Your lieutenant seems like a decent guy."

"He is."

"It occurred to me it could have been some kind of burglar," David said. "The girl walked in on him—"

"It occurred to me," Quist said. "What's missing?"

"I—we haven't had a chance to look very thoroughly."

"So look. Did Peggy keep jewelry up here?"

"Costume jewelry," David said. "We never spent money on the real thing."

"Maybe your thief wouldn't know the difference. Look."

Peggy, without a word, turned from the windows and went to the bureau. She took a leather box out of a top drawer and opened it.

"Nothing seems to be gone," she said, after a moment's search.

Nothing would be gone, Quist told himself. The burglar

theory was a vain hope on his part, on David's part.

"You know anything about Abigail Tyler, David?"

"No. I left Dabney when I was eighteen years old—living there, I mean. I don't recall any Tylers. I know I never saw the girl before she came to the studio last night. But she had a note from Old Nick."

"Walter Nichols?"

"Yes. 'My girl Friday,' he wrote. 'Give her a break.' So there was no time then, and I knew there'd be no time at the party. Peggy suggested breakfast. I knew we'd have to stay to the very end, so we gave her Peggy's key and told her to come on ahead if she got bored with the party. Peggy called the doorman to forewarn him."

"She was a child," Quist said, cold anger gripping him again. "She left the party early because she was embarrassed. Her dress strap broke while she was dancing with me. Just a child!"

"I suppose we should get in touch with Mr. Nichols," Peggy said.

"I've arranged for that," Quist said. "You don't know anything about the girl's family?"

"I've told you, I never heard of her until tonight," David said. "We didn't have any kind of talk. That was to come later at breakfast."

"So you didn't know Abigail, and she didn't know you except by reputation—and maybe a little hometown gossip. Could she have dug up something you couldn't afford to have spilled?"

David stared at Quist, his eyes wide. "Are you suggesting that I—that Peggy and I—?"

"Someone may suggest it. Someone who's already trying to stir up trouble for you."

"Who? What trouble?" Peggy asked.

"I didn't get a chance to tell you about it, Peg," David

said. "Some nut writing letters to Micky Grant and Jake Betz and Laverick, demanding that they drop me. Meaningless— except Laverick is bothered by it. I'm supposed to be at his office in a couple of hours." David was looking straight at Quist as he said this. He hadn't mentioned the snapshot that went with the letters. He was, silently, pleading with Quist not to mention it to Peggy; not to mention it until they could talk. That talk must come soon, Quist thought. Very soon.

Kreevich appeared in the doorway, knocked politely, and came in. "Perhaps I can relieve you all of certain tensions," he said. "The medical examiner's man assures me that Abigail Tyler has been dead from four to five hours—the longer time more likely. It's now eight o'clock. That would place her death at sometime between three and four this morning. I've checked with the security people at the Beaumont, Mr. Hale. They assure me that you and Mrs. Hale didn't leave there until about six-thirty. They had a man watching you all evening to protect you from crackpots and autograph hounds. He provides you and Mrs. Hale with unbreakable alibis."

"Had you—had you suspected us?" Peggy asked in a small voice.

"I'd suspect my own mother till I'd checked out on her, Mrs. Hale. So, at least we don't have to stalk each other like unfriendly dogs." The detective changed his tack. He held out his hand and opened his clenched fist. "Do you recognize this? Does it belong to you, Mrs. Hale? Mr. Hale?"

There it was. Another copy of the snapshot—the tall man with the black glasses and the blond boy. The burglar had vanished.

Peggy's pleasant Irish face was screwed up in a puzzled frown. "It's not ours, Lieutenant," she said. "I never saw it before. Where did it come from?"

"The Tyler girl was gripping it in her left hand," Kreevich

said. "We had to pry open her fingers to see what it was. Mean anything to you, Mr. Hale?"

David opened his mouth and closed it as if he couldn't get breath enough to speak.

"There's no point in pretending you haven't seen it before, David," Quist said. He wasn't comfortable. If he didn't speak he would betray one friend, Kreevich; if he did he would be denying David's unspoken plea for silence. "That picture has been floating around all night, Mark. Not that particular one, but copies of it." He reached into his inside pocket and brought out his own letter. He handed it to Kreevich.

The detective glanced at the snapshot and then read the letter aloud. " 'You must be dying to solve the mystery, Mr. Quist. The snapshot is really your first clue. It could be called the long and the short of it.' " Kreevich looked up, his pale eyes quite cold. "What mystery? What is this, Julian?"

"At least three other copies of that picture are in existence," Quist said. "They were enclosed in identical letters to Michael Grant, the president of the International Television Network, Gerald Laverick of Laverick Enterprises, who is the main sponsor of David's show, and Jake Betz of Betz and Smallwood, the advertising agency that is handling the account. The letter says, roughly, that if they don't want the roof to cave in they'd better investigate the story that photograph will lead to. The letter writer says he will never let them get away with promoting David."

"And what story will the snapshot lead us to, Mr. Hale?" Kreevich asked.

David shook his head slowly, doggedly. "I haven't any idea at all," he said. "I never saw the snapshot until earlier tonight when Micky Grant showed me the one he'd received."

"You know who the people are in the picture?" Kreevich asked.

David stared at it, not speaking. Peggy was suddenly beside him, her arm slipped through his. When David did speak it was not an answer to the detective's question. "Did you have your letter all the while we were talking with Micky, Julian?"

"No. It was waiting for me when I got home. A messenger delivered it like the others." He turned to Kreevich. "Have you looked at that snapshot closely? It's a copy of a very old one. You can see where it's faded, and there's some kind of a stain in the lower left-hand corner—a flaw in the original negative, perhaps."

"They have techniques for copying old photographs and eliminating the fading and the flaws," Kreevich said.

"Maybe our letter sender didn't know that," Quist said. "I'm more inclined to think he wanted us to recognize it as old—fifteen, twenty, twenty-five years old." He looked at David. "Twenty-five years ago you'd have been about the same age as that boy in the picture, David."

"Twenty-five years ago I would have been thirteen," David said.

"And you don't recognize the boy or the man?" Kreevich asked.

David appeared to study the snapshot closely, but somehow Quist knew he was pretending.

"The man's face is turned away—the black glasses," David said. "The boy—?" He shrugged.

"You don't have any idea how this letter writer thinks he can damage you?" Kreevich asked.

"There's nothing," David said, very quietly. "My life is an open book—to coin a cliché."

"You didn't have a copy of this snapshot? No letter to you?"

"No to both questions," David said.

"The Tyler girl didn't find this picture—say, downstairs

on your living room table—pick it up to look at it—just as she was shot?"

"There wasn't a copy of it here. I never saw it till Micky Grant showed us his copy about two-thirty this morning."

" 'Us'?"

"Julian and me."

"The girl either found the picture here, brought it with her, or was given it to look at by the person who shot her," Kreevich said. "Which way do you like it, Mr. Hale?"

"She didn't find it here. It wasn't here to be found," David said. "Whether she brought it with her, or it was shown to her when she got here by someone who'd broken in—"

"Or it was planted on her to keep us interested," Quist said.

"The killer came through your garden, Mr. Hale," Kreevich said. "There's a pane of glass broken out of one of the French doors so that he could get at the inside lock. My men are going over the back yard. I suspect we'll find the killer came and went that way. The doorman never saw anyone but the Tyler girl, whom he'd been told might come and who had Mrs. Hale's key as ID." Kreevich frowned. "He didn't hear the shot, either. But about the time we think it happened he was out on the pavement trying to help a drunken neighbor of yours out of a taxi."

David glanced at his watch. "I've got to be thinking about going to the meeting at Laverick's office," he said. "I need to get out of these evening clothes. . . . Is there any reason I can't go to the meeting, Lieutenant? It's really quite important, particularly in view of—of this."

"I'll need a detailed statement from both you and Mrs. Hale, but that can be done later in the day," Kreevich said. "Since you're not suspects."

"I've been asked to go to Laverick's too," Quist said. "I'll wait for you."

"Fifteen minutes to shave and clean up," David said.

Quist followed Kreevich down the little spiral staircase to the living room. The Homicide crew was busy with cameras and fingerprint equipment, but Abigail—poor little Abigail—was gone. Kreevich turned his bright eyes on Quist.

"What's your friend and client hiding from me, Julian?" he asked.

"You think he's hiding something?"

"Oh, for God sake, Julian, you've heard enough lies told in your time to have an ear for it. I didn't blast him because I think he's trying to hide whatever it is from his wife, among others. She seems like a nice woman."

"She's a doll."

"I figured I'd waste a lot of time trying to pry it out of him and that you'd tell me if you knew."

"I don't know."

"Then persuade him to tell you, and in a hurry!" Kreevich said. "Let's not you and I kid around with a burglar theory. The girl was followed here, or someone who knew she was coming got here ahead of her and was waiting for her. Whatever that snapshot may tell us about David Hale, it also has something to do with someone's motive for killing Abigail Tyler. She was hanging on to it for dear life when she was killed."

"Why didn't the killer take it if that was what he was after?"

"Probably because he wanted us to find it," Kreevich said. "He wants you to run down the story behind that picture. He says so in his note to you. But if you don't he wants us to run it down. Somebody doesn't like your friend and client quite a lot."

"I'll do what I can," Quist said.

"You'd better bring him along to Headquarters after your

meeting," Kreevich said. "If he hasn't told you what it's all about by then, I'll have to try my talents on him."

"Can I use the phone?" Quist asked.

"You done with the telephone, Harry?" Kreevich asked one of the fingerprint men.

"All clear."

Quist dialed his apartment and Lydia answered. "No mistake?" she asked. "It was Abigail?"

"No mistake. And she was gripping one of those snapshots in a dead hand."

"Julian!"

"Did you reach Walter Nichols?"

"Yes. He's a thunderstorm of a man, Julian. Rage—grief, I think. He will personally find the sonofabitch who did it and cut him into small, unappetizing pieces."

"The girl's family?"

"He'll notify them. He anticipates they will drive down to New York at once. They'll call me when they get here to find out where Abigail is. That should be not sooner than midafternoon. The father teaches in the local high school."

"Did he happen to mention how long they'd lived in Dabney?"

"They came there about ten years ago," Lydia said.

Lydia always asked the right questions, Quist thought. "I'm off to Laverick's office with David," he said. "I think I'd like Dan to join me there. Will you call him?"

"Of course. Anything else I can do?"

"Stay available," Quist said.

Soft laughter on the other end. "Don't I always, darling?"

As Quist put down the phone, David, looking darkly handsome in a blue tropical worsted suit, came down from the bedroom. He looked relieved to see that Abigail was gone.

"My wife will be upstairs if you need her, Lieutenant," he said.

"I can get her statement," Kreevich said. "I'll want yours when your meeting is over. I've asked Julian to bring you to my office."

"Certainly," David said.

Quist and David walked out onto the street and hailed a taxi. David sat in one corner, looking straight ahead of him at the back of the driver's head. The glass partition made private conversation possible, but David seemed to want to avoid it, as if he knew what was coming.

"I don't know what you're hiding from me, chum," Quist said. "Whatever it is I guess you're hiding it from Peggy, too. Kreevich thinks you're stalling about the snapshot. He's giving you the chance to talk to me. If you don't, he can make it tough."

David drew a deep, quavering breath as though he were strangling for oxygen. "I don't know why you don't believe me, Julian," he said. "What have I done to you to make you distrust me?"

"Whoever sent out these letters, David, knows that sooner or later someone will identify that photograph and, at the same time, discover why it can be damaging to you. If it can damage you, you know why. It isn't that you've done anything to me to make me distrust you. It's just that it doesn't make sense any other way. You have to know what that picture means."

"I've told you and Micky and your cop friend—I never saw that picture before last night. I swear that's the truth, Julian."

"All right, I'll buy that," Quist said. "But you do know who the people are in the picture."

It was obviously a moment of decision for David, and, right or wrong, he made it. "I don't recognize either the man or the boy," he said.

Quist leaned forward and tapped on the glass partition. The driver opened the little change hole in the glass. "Let me out here," Quist said.

David's hand closed hard on his wrist. His hand and arm were trembling. "Please, Julian! I need you—need your help!"

"Then tell me who the people are in the picture."

The cab had pulled up at the curb.

"*I don't know!* But I need you at this meeting, Julian. I need you to convince Laverick that I'm clear on this murder thing. I need you to make him see that it won't hurt my image as an interviewer and commentator. You don't think it will, do you?"

"It will probably enlarge your audience," Quist said. "It's what will happen when they find out who the man and the boy in the picture are and why they can hurt you. I can't promise Laverick that won't damage you. How can I when you won't tell me what it is? David, I've done my job for you. You're launched. You'll make your own success or failure from here on in." He reached for the cab door.

David's grip on his arm tightened. "Please, Julian!"

Quist leaned back against the seat. He looked at this man he'd accepted as a friend; his eyes narrowed. "If I know Gerald Laverick, he'll have some of his people run that picture down. He isn't a man who'll take anyone's word for anything. If it can wreck you, as someone obviously thinks it can, there's no way I can help without the whole truth from you."

"I've told you the truth!"

"Oh David, David, David. I told you last night I was as safe as your priest or your psychiatrist. Tell me the truth. I don't have to pass it on, but I have to know how to help."

"I swear to you, Julian—"

"Suppose I set out to find it for myself? The truth? Will that leave us friends?"

"Of course."

Quist sighed, and gestured to the driver to keep on going.

FOUR

"We are one large family," Gerald Laverick said. "We must hang together like one large family."

"Or we will all hang separately," an amused voice said from the corner of the room.

Laverick turned his head, a shaven skull over which skin was stretched. His pale blue eyes were cold as two newly minted dimes. He spoke with the careful precision of a man who has practiced for a long time to perfect the handling of expensive dentures. He was, Quist thought, the perfect embodiment of a comic-strip heavy, except that there was nothing at all funny about the power he wielded. He could wipe out whole businesses, corporations, even governments simply by picking up the telephone at his elbow. Laverick Enterprises manipulated a substantial portion of the American economy. On this morning in the board room of the company's main offices on Wall Street Gerald Laverick was in a position to wipe out eight or ten people gathered there with no more effort than it would have taken him to exterminate a fly with a fly swatter.

"You will have your opportunity to talk later, Mr. Brickley," Laverick said to the man in the corner of the room. "If there is anything to talk about." The pale eyes moved to David who was standing beside Quist at the door. "If Mr. Hale has become a suspect in a murder case, there will be nothing to talk about. You would save us a great deal of speech-making, Mr. Hale, if you would tell us exactly what your status is."

"I am completely in the clear, Mr. Laverick, as far as the police are concerned," David said. "My wife and I were still at the Beaumont when this unfortunate girl was shot in our apartment. The police are satisfied."

"Perhaps you'd care to tell me what this girl was doing in your apartment," Laverick said.

David explained. While he talked Quist looked around the elegant board room at Laverick's "family." Except for Dan Garvey, Quist's business partner, and Laverick's cool-looking private secretary, a Miss Atwater, and his harried-looking personal lawyer, one Jason Crown, and a stone-faced bodyguard who stood behind Laverick's chair, everyone else was connected in one way or another with David's new show, Night Talk. Jake Betz and Terry Smallwood represented the multimillion-dollar advertising account. Night Talk could keep Betz and Smallwood alive for the next five years, a lovely cushion in a world of cutthroat competition. There was Micky Grant, who looked as if he certainly had never gone to bed that night or morning. He had cut himself shaving. There was the producer for the network, the studio director, the writers and researchers. There was a short, fat little man who was easing his way along the rear wall of the room to stand by David. He was George Walberg, known as Pudge to his intimates, who was David's gofor—go for a cup of coffee, go for the mail, go for a clean shirt, go for broke if necessary. Pudge Walberg was as loyal as a pet spaniel, almost worshipful. David could have asked Pudge to lie down in front of an advancing steam roller and Pudge would have done it without question. His not to reason why; his but to do or die.

You could almost smell fear in the room, Quist thought.

All of these people connected with Night Talk had felt they were secure for the next five years. Now that old bastard at the head of the table could destroy all that if David had left him a loophole—a violation of the morals clause in his contract. It's one thing not to get a job, but something else again to lose it after you've thought you were in the winner's circle. Some of them had probably spent money they might not now be going to get.

Quist, studying the tense faces, was listening to David. He was telling how he and Peggy had found Abigail dead, how they had called Quist for help, how the police had come. What he did not tell was that Kreevich had found a copy of that photograph clutched in Abigail's dead hand.

When David had finished, Laverick's pale eyes fastened on Quist. "What is the opinion of our expert on public relations?" he asked, in his thin, cold voice.

"Lieutenant Kreevich will have made it quite clear to the media by now that there isn't a shred of suspicion attached to the Hales," Quist said. "The only possible effect on Night Talk may be that you'll have more viewers on Monday night, when you start next week's cycle of shows, than you would have had. The most obvious explanation of what happened to the Tyler girl is that she surprised a thief in David's apartment. It's a tragic thing. She was a nice kid. But David never saw her before in his life until last night."

"She came from his hometown," Laverick said. His eyelids never seemed to blink.

"Her family only came to Dabney ten years ago," Quist said, "long after David had migrated to Hollywood. He didn't know them. There's no past connection. This unhappy murder can't, in my judgment, have any effect on Night Talk."

You could almost hear collective breaths being exhaled.

"So we come to the reason this meeting was called for in the first place," Laverick said. "Threatening letters and a photograph."

So here it was. Quist was aware that David took a quick look at him, but he kept turned away.

"Well, Mr. Hale?" Laverick asked.

"I really don't have anything to say, Mr. Laverick," David said. "I have never seen that photograph before. I saw it for the first time last night when Micky Grant showed me the one he'd received. I don't know what it's supposed to mean to me—or to you. I don't feel threatened by it because it's meaningless."

"Somebody thinks he has the goods on you, Hale," Laverick said.

"What goods? I have lived a very unsensational life," David said. "There aren't any secret corridors and blind alleys in it that I'm aware of."

"Not altogether unsensational," Laverick said. He was making a steeple out of his square-tipped fingers. "There was —perhaps I should say 'is'—Janice Trail. Did you, by the way, invite her to last night's party?"

"Of course not."

"I rather imagined you wouldn't have," Laverick said. He leaned forward to wag a finger at David. He looked, Quist thought, like a hanging judge in the old frontier days. He moistened his lips as though there were some sort of sensual pleasure in threatening David. "Be certain, Hale, that I wouldn't hesitate thirty seconds to blow this whole adventure sky high if I found you'd lied to me."

David stood up to it pretty well. A muscle rippled along the line of his jaw. He was fighting anger. "I happen to know you had me very thoroughly investigated before you signed the contracts, Mr. Laverick."

"You can bet on that," Laverick said. He leaned back and

turned his unblinking eyes on Jason Crown, his lawyer. "In view of these letters and these photographs, Jason, is there anything you may have passed over too quickly?"

Crown was a handsome, almost actorish-looking man in his early fifties. He still had a well-conditioned body, Quist saw, but the lines in his face and around his eyes suggested unbearable pressures which he compensated for with too much alcohol. You could be driven to drink if you worked for a man like Laverick.

"There is nothing, sir," Crown said. "And I can assure you the investigation was thorough."

"It better have been, Jason," the old man said. He turned his gaze to Quist. "You are a connoisseur of the sensational, Mr. Quist. What is your opinion of these letters and the photograph? You make a speciality of sifting the dirt out of human histories, don't you?"

"Do you mind," Quist asked quietly, "if before I answer your question I tell you that I find you an offensive old prick?"

Miss Atwater and Crown looked as if they couldn't believe what they'd heard. The bodyguard's face turned rock hard. The rest of the people seemed to freeze except for one.

"Hear, hear!" Dan Garvey said, grinning at his boss and friend.

Laverick smiled. "You are the first person who has talked back to me for twenty-five years, Quist. I find it refreshing. How would you like to come to work for Laverick Enterprises?"

Quist smiled back at him. "I would loathe it," he said.

Laverick nodded. "I'm sure everyone here will buy you a drink when you leave—if they think I'm not looking. Well?"

"Well, what?"

"Your opinion of the letters and the photograph."

"I could deliver you a lecture on the subject," Quist said.

"I have time," Laverick said, "if you will stay on the question."

"We are living in pretty frightening times," Quist said. "We are dominated by men who care only for power, and they acquire their power from the even more powerful, men like yourself, Laverick, who are the submerged portion of the iceberg."

"Oh, dear, is it to be a lecture on morals, Quist?"

"On the lack of morals and the result that produces," Quist said. "The countermove is terror, Mr. Laverick. No one can get heard today without stealing people, or stealing people's reputations. Political kidnapings are one sample. People hijacked on planes and threatened to death unless friends of the hijackers are released from political prisons. Then there is the destruction of reputations—the reputations of dissenters—by men in power, through the misuse of government agencies, bribery, illegal wiretaps, burglary. One crime is countered by another crime."

"I find myself just a little bored, Mr. Quist," Laverick said.

"That's half the lecture," Quist said. "There's an interesting thing about these letters and the picture that goes with them. David hasn't received one. David hasn't been threatened, hasn't been asked for blackmail money, hasn't been urged to use his show, Night Talk, to help someone or attack someone. I find myself wondering if there isn't someone else who ought to be frightened, not David. Do you know who those people are in the picture, Laverick? Is someone warning you to watch your step? Or you, Mr. Betz? Or you, Micky? This is a very complex operation involving Laverick Enterprises, a national network, a giant advertising agency. The only person involved who has recently been examined closely is David. Clean, says Mr. Crown. Clean, say the researchers in my office. Clean in the murder of Abigail Tyler, say the police. He is, you might say, the original Mr.

Clean. Has anybody else been under such a microscope recently? I would guess not. But I have to think somebody in this complex knows what that picture means, what it can do to him when the meaning becomes clear, or to his particular business. And the man who sent it knows. And so it's my opinion that we are dealing with some kind of Judas freak within this complex and that David is being used as a red herring."

"Judas freak?" Laverick asked.

"A Judas—a traitor—a seller-outer," Quist said. "In the gobbledegook of modern slang, a 'freak' is someone who is dedicated to, who loves to, an *aficionado*. A Judas freak. A man who loves to betray."

The room was silent for a moment, and then Laverick stood up. Instantly Miss Atwater and Crown stood. The bodyguard moved toward the door.

"Interesting theory, Mr. Quist," Laverick said. "It is now close to noon on Saturday. Night Talk doesn't go on again till Monday night. Let us say it is still on, unless something turns up over the weekend to convince me otherwise. But I promise you all something. My father used to say that if you want to find the cheese turn the mice loose. Well, I'm turning the mice loose, gentlemen. There's going to be an investigation of this whole situation that will make the FBI look like amateurs. So, have a nice weekend, everybody."

Most of the people connected with Night Talk crowded around David. He was their boy, their golden goose. He had weathered the storm for the moment.

Quist found himself in an outer reception room with Dan Garvey. Physically, these two were complete opposites in coloring—Quist a golden blond, blue-eyed, tall and slender; Garvey very dark, as tall as Quist but a good twenty pounds heavier, all bone and muscle. Garvey had been a professional football player of great promise when he'd been struck down by a knee injury. He'd gone into sports broadcasting and then met Quist somewhere, been persuaded to become a member of Julian Quist Associates. People in the sports world today draw such enormous salaries that they need special promotion to earn what they get paid.

"Great speech you made in there," Dan said. "Do you happen to believe any of it?"

"I don't know for sure, Daniel," Quist said, frowning. "Things I didn't mention. I got one of those letters and a picture. I'll show it to you later. That poor Tyler kid was clutching one of the pictures in her dead hand when Kreevich got there."

"Brother!"

"I think David is lying about the picture. I think he knows who the people are in it."

"But if that's so—"

"Damn it, Dan, the ball game is over if someone has something on him! Why wouldn't he fight instead of lying about it? I have a strange feeling he may be protecting somebody else."

"Who?"

"No notion. Not Peggy, I think. She drew a complete blank when Kreevich showed her the snapshot, unless she's the greatest living actress."

"And Mr. Clean won't come clean with you?"

"Nope. I gave him every chance."

"So drop it. We've done our job for him. Let him get out of his own cesspool."

Quist shook his head. "It's got me so goddamned curious, Daniel. And there's our little Abbie. I liked that kid. She was fresh, and young, and different. She could blush, which is unheard of in this day and age. It's all tied together somehow, and I'm not going to enjoy looking at myself in my shaving mirror if I don't find the answers."

Micky Grant came out of the board room, a wide grin on his Irish face. "I don't suppose anybody has called that old prick an old prick in his whole life," he said. "Thanks, Julian, for standing up to him."

"Not difficult," Quist said. "He hasn't got anything on me and I'm not dependent on him."

Micky's smile seemed to freeze a little. "He's smashed governments in his time, dad. If he decided to crush you, just for the fun of it—"

"Dan and I will enjoy the exercise," Quist said, and knew as he spoke that Micky was right. Laverick could be mortally dangerous.

David came out of the board room surrounded by Tom and Rita Brickley and the faithful gofor, Pudge Walberg. Tom Brickley was the glib young man who had suggested they might all hang separately at the start of the meeting with Laverick. Tom and his wife Rita were the heads of the writing and research staff for Night Talk. They were young, precocious, very mod in their lifestyle, brashly unafraid of anything they might have to face in life, but certainly relieved to know that Night Talk was safe for the time being.

Rita Brickley gave Quist an appraising look from under her long black lashes. "For the first time in my life I find myself interested in an older man," she said.

"You were real cool in there, man," Tom Brickley said. "I have a feeling the old man enjoyed it. He's been surrounded for so long by nothing but behind-kissers." He turned to David. "I didn't get a chance to tell you, pal, that Janice Trail's agent called to let us know she was available as a guest on your show." He laughed. "I told him I didn't think the sponsor would buy the lady."

"Bitch!" It was a whisper from Pudge Walberg. He reached out a warm, moist hand and placed it on Quist's.

"Thanks," he said. "David needed you in there."

Quist moved his hand away, feeling there was something unpleasantly intimate about the touch. He wondered if Pudge could persuade David he was walking a dangerous tightrope by not telling the whole truth.

Police headquarters was only a few blocks from Laverick's office. Quist asked Dan to call Lydia and suggest that the three of them have lunch at Willard's Back Yard in about an hour. Then he and David set out on foot for Kreevich's office.

David was silent again. He walked, looking straight ahead of him. His eyes were dark and troubled.

"I held back some of the facts, David," Quist said. "There seemed no point in giving Laverick something extra to club you with."

"I know. I appreciate it. Of course Kreevich may let the cat out of the bag about your letter, and the picture the girl was holding."

"And he may not," Quist said. "It's not his style to tell the press everything he knows. He's after a killer, not publicity. But sometime, chum, you're going to have to come clean."

No more denials. Just silence.

Kreevich was in his office, a paper cup of cold coffee on the desk beside him. His eyes asked Quist a question, and Quist shook his head. The detective's eyes narrowed.

"I'm going to turn you over to a police stenographer, Mr. Hale," he said. "I want a detailed statement from you about your first meeting with Miss Tyler when she came to the studio last night. What she asked you, what you arranged with her, the invitation to breakfast, the passing of a key to her. Who else knew about the arrangement beside your wife? There was the doorman Mrs. Hale phoned with instructions. Who else? Any other contact you had with Miss Tyler during the evening."

"There was none. I saw her dancing with a couple of

people early on at the party. You danced with her, didn't you, Julian?"

"Yes."

"I didn't notice when she left the party," David said. "But the doorman can tell you when she got to our place."

"He has," Kreevich said. "Just before three o'clock. So, then I want a detailed account of your arrival home, what you found, what you did before you called Quist, what you did after you called and until the patrol car cops arrived. Don't leave anything out."

"I understand."

"Make yourself comfortable. I'll send the stenographer in to you right away. Coffee?"

David glanced at the paper cup. "I think not."

"Wise man," Kreevich said, with a faint little smile. "Talk to you, Julian?"

Quist left David and went out of the office with Kreevich. The detective took him to another office a few doors down the hall.

"He wouldn't talk?" Kreevich asked.

"No. I pressured him, but no talk."

"We can try to get it out of him here before we let him go."

Quist frowned. "Somehow I don't think it will work, Mark. I have a theory since I last saw you—that he may be protecting someone else and not himself. He may need to contact that person, maneuver a little, before he'll loosen up. He's basically a very decent guy, Mark. The kind of a guy who'd run risks for a friend."

"Or his wife? Or a girl?"

"Aren't women classified as friends in your world, Mark?"

"Let's leave the vaudeville routines for later," Kreevich said, sharply. "I have two facts for you since I last saw you. The Tyler girl was shot in the head with a German Luger. Could be a relic from way back—maybe a souvenir from

World War Two. Suggest anything?"

"No."

"Well, hang on to it for a moment. Our camera expert here agrees with you. He thinks—and I'll skip the technical jargon—that the snapshot from which the pictures we have were copied is a good twenty to twenty-five years old. So we have a gun that dates back to World War Two, and a picture that may have been taken about nineteen forty-nine. Department of ancient history, you might say. The Tyler girl wasn't born then. She was twenty-two. What could the picture have meant to her?"

"So we go back to some early beginnings," Quist said.

"Beginnings which are where?"

Quist took one of his long, thin cigars out of the leather case he carried in the inside pocket of his jacket. He lit it. "Have you any objection if Lydia and I take a trip to Dabney, Vermont, and nose around a little?"

Kreevich relaxed. "I was hoping you'd suggest it," he said.

Willard's Back Yard is a delightful place to lunch in the summertime. There is, literally, an awning-covered back yard, decorated with potted shrubs and flowers.

Standing in the entrance to the outdoor area Quist saw Lydia seated at a corner table with Garvey. Though he knew she was his, he always felt a little churning in his gut whenever he saw her with some other man. He would have denied with his last breath that he could be so unsophisticated as to feel jealousy. He started toward the table, saw her face light up with pleasure, and felt secure again.

He sat down beside Lydia and reached out to touch her knee. Her eyes were the color of violets. He ordered a double Jack Daniels on the rocks with a splash of water, muttering something about catching up with them. Lydia had a vermouth poured over shaved ice, Garvey a very dry martini.

They would all have the lobster Newberg and a green salad —after a second round of drinks.

Quist brought his friends up-to-date on Kreevich's findings about the gun and the age of the snapshot.

"Twenty-five years ago is pretty dusty territory for all of us," Garvey said. "I was playing fullback on the Clark Street Midgets, age ten." He grinned at Lydia. "You were still getting your meals out of baby-food jars."

"I had a plastic duck in my bathtub," Lydia said.

"Lucky duck," Quist said. "I was playing Long John Silver in a prep school dramatization of *Treasure Island*. But somebody had a souvenir German gun that was to be used to murder a girl who wasn't yet born. And somebody took a picture of a man and a boy which we are led to believe can destroy David Hale a quarter of a century later."

"Or destroy somebody else if your theory that David is protecting somebody else holds water," Dan said.

Quist sipped the drink the waiter brought him and looked at his lovely lady. "How would you like to spend a couple of days in the Green Mountains? David was still going to school in Dabney twenty-five years ago. Pudge Walberg, too. I have a feeling Dabney is where it all began."

"I'd like it fine," Lydia said. "You've never made love to me in Vermont."

"We could drive up this afternoon, spend Sunday and Monday there," Quist said. "Come back on Tuesday."

"You have half a dozen important appointments on Monday and Tuesday," Lydia said.

"I'll have Connie cancel the ones Dan and Bobby can't handle."

Garvey's face had clouded. "Maybe we'd better order that second round of drinks," he said. "I have the feeling we are about to enjoy an unpleasantness." He was looking toward the entrance to the back yard. So were most of Willard's customers. Framed in the doorway was the blond and voluptuous Janice Trail and her escort, who was Max Robson, the critic with the Fu Manchu mustache. Robson was talking to the headwaiter, and pointing to an empty table next to Quist's.

People try to behave themselves in the presence of public glamor but Janice Trail was a little much for Willard's customers. There was a buzz of excited conversation to go with open staring, and one woman reached out, almost hysterically, to touch the movie star as she followed the waiter toward the table. She was wearing an apricot-colored dress that hung loosely around her full-breasted figure. It was what in the trade was called the "tent silhouette." It gave the impression, quite intentionally Quist imagined, that she had nothing on under it. Strong men were intended to swoon.

Max Robson was smiling his white, toothpaste smile as he approached.

"Hail, oh brilliant ones!" he said, and caricatured a deep bow of respect. "I suspect a serious council of war. Has your cleverly fabricated genius been arrested for murder yet?"

The headwaiter was holding a chair for Janice Trail, and as she sat down her wide greenish eyes were fixed on Lydia. Was she sitting too close to another glamorous woman?

"Has not and will not be, Max-baby," Garvey said.

"Does Gerald Laverick own the Homicide Bureau along with the rest of his possessions?" Robson asked. "By the way, Quist, I don't believe you've met Janice Trail."

Quist gave the lady an almost imperceptible little nod of greeting. He made no effort to introduce his friends.

"And this, Janice, my love, is Miss Lydia Morton," Robson said, "who is rumored to belong exclusively to the Great Man. And Dan Garvey, who dreams of being a professional pugilist."

Quist raised his hand and beckoned to the headwaiter,

who came quickly to his side.

"Will you be good enough to find us another table," Quist asked, "or another table for Mr. Robson. I find him offensive." It was said loud and clear so that other people could hear it without any difficulty.

Robson's face turned a dark, angry red. "I don't think I have to take that from you, Quist," he said.

"So go away and you won't have to," Quist said. "If it comes to a showdown, we can heave you bodily out onto the street. Only if you insist, of course."

"Please, gentlemen, please," Janice Trail said, obviously enjoying herself. "You do have a wicked tongue, Max, darling. And I did so want to tell Mr. Quist what a brilliant job he's done in promoting David. I've always heard you can't make bricks out of straw, but you've accomplished something very like that, Mr. Quist. Unfortunately, David won't be able to stand up under the pressures of five shows a week, even if he can survive an assortment of scandals. He hasn't the intellect for it. He's really a very shallow fellow."

"David is in the clear on last night's tragedy," Garvey said. "He has survived his affair with you, Miss Trail. What other scandals did you have in mind?"

Quist stood up.

"We all have a past of one sort or another," Janice Trail said. "Sooner or later David's will catch up with him. Bear in mind, I know him as intimately or better than any other person on earth. You've set up a hollow man to carry a giant load."

Garvey, surprisingly, said: " 'Heaven has no rage like love to hatred turned,/ Nor hell a fury like a woman scorned.' William Congreve."

"Watch it, chum," Quist said. "Your Phi Beta Kappa key is showing." He turned to the waiter. "Be good enough to take our drinks to the bar. When you have another table we'll take it—if we still have an appetite for lunch." He herded Lydia and Garvey toward the bar and then turned back to Robson and Miss Trail. "We can play word games forever without damaging each other, Max. But if it ever gets to be more than shadowboxing, you'd better be well prepared. I'll find the ammunition to blow you sky-high if I have to." His bright blue eyes shifted to the woman. "Your dream of getting on David's show and sniping at him in public is just that, Miss Trail—a dream. The sponsor won't buy a dead love affair as entertainment."

The offices of Julian Quist Associates were not open for business on a summer Saturday afternoon, but it wasn't unusual for people to be working there. Quist let himself into the reception room with his personal key. The place always seemed deserted to him when the bright and handsome Miss Gloria Chard wasn't seated at her circular desk directing traffic. The modern paintings on the pastel walls looked somehow deserted and lonely.

Quist walked down the back corridor to his private office and there he found his personal secretary, Miss Constance Parmalee. Connie, her eyes shaded by tinted granny glasses, was seated at Quist's desk where she'd obviously been phoning.

"What are you doing here, luv?" Quist asked.

"I thought you might need me. I heard the news about the murder on the radio. Bobby Hilliard told me about last night —the letters, the snapshots."

"You are something!" Quist said. "You could help. I'd like to find a place for me and Lydia to stay in Dabney, Vermont, for the next three nights."

"I've got two rooms for you at the Dabney House," Connie said, matter-of-factly. "Very old, but elegant and good food."

"What the hell made you think I'd be going there?"

"I like to think I know how your mind works, boss."

"I repeat, you are something, Connie. Would you call the Automobile Club and get me a road route to Dabney, plus what they think my chances of getting adequate gasoline are?"

"I've arranged for Ed O'Brian to fly you up this afternoon. I'm to let him know when. I've arranged a rental car for you which will be waiting for you at the little airport near Dabney. I've cancelled your appointment with the Koehler people on Monday and Lester Thompson on Tuesday. I think Dan and Bobby can handle everyone else."

Quist shook his head, slowly. "My God, what a wife you'd make for someone," he said.

Connie looked demurely down at her notes. "I guess I'm just not the marrying kind," she said.

He knew, and she knew he knew, that no one on earth mattered to her but one Julian Quist.

"I'm terribly grateful to you, luv," he said. This tall red-haired girl with the high cheekbones, the wide, generous mouth, and the fabulous legs was a great deal more than the kind of office computer that she pretended to be, and Quist knew it very well.

He walked over to the perfectly equipped little bar in the far corner of the office and poured himself a short drink.

"David's problems are David's," he said. "We've done our job for him, and since he doesn't choose to come clean about what's bothering him, there's nothing we can do for him. But that girl, Abigail Tyler! I was dancing with her when her dress strap broke, exposing an innocent little apple of a breast. She ran for the powder room, overcome with embarrassment. She never came back, and walked straight into a killer's gun. I want to square her account for her, Connie."

"That's Kreevich's job, isn't it?" Connie asked, her eyes lowered.

"For some reason I feel a personal obligation. She was such a nice, wide-open kid."

Connie stood up and moved toward the door of her own office. "Lydia told me about it this morning," she said. "I was to take a call from the girl's family if Lydia wasn't here. I—I took it on myself to make a minor inquiry about it, boss."

"Oh?"

"Lydia had asked the woman attendant in the powder room if Abigail had asked for a needle and thread. She hadn't."

"I know."

"I got the woman's home phone number from the security officer at the Beaumont. A Mrs. Martha Trout. I asked her if she remembered seeing Abigail, needle or no needle. She didn't. There was a reason."

"What reason?"

"There were several women in the powder room about that time. One of them was Janice Trail. Everyone was concentrating on America's sex queen. Mrs. Trout told me that a man could have walked in and gone to the john and nobody would have noticed."

"Proving what, luv?"

"There's a key question you and Kreevich are asking, isn't there? Where did Abigail get the snapshot she was holding when you found her? Could she have heard something there, or found the snapshot there in the powder room and split as fast as she could?"

"That would mean the snapshot meant something to her, and she wasn't born when it was taken."

"But she comes from Dabney. That's why I was sure you'd be going there."

Quist finished his drink and put down his glass. He told Connie about the luncheon encounter with Janice Trail and Max Robson.

"I can understand Janice Trail's wanting to hurt David," he said. "But murdering that kid from the country? Besides, she was still at the party when we left, which was about the time Abigail was being killed."

"A hit?" Connie suggested.

"Professional?"

"Could be," Connie said.

Quist frowned at the cigar he took out of his pocket case. "Max Robson is a professional sadist," he said. "He enjoys chopping up people in the public eye. But killing Abigail just doesn't make sense."

"I could do a rundown on both of them while you're gone, Trail and Robson," Connie said, "to see if there's any remote connection with Dabney, Vermont."

"You really are a doll, Connie," Quist said.

She gave him a very faint smile. "Thank you, sir," she said.

Quist had used Ed O'Brian's charter plane service many times before. The plane was a Cessna, and it landed Quist and Lydia at a little airfield just north of Dabney at about six o'clock that afternoon. The pilot was instructed to come back for them on Tuesday afternoon.

An attendant at the small office building on the field pointed out a small, compact black sedan parked alongside the runway. He gave them directions to the Dabney House.

The blue-green hills were unbelievably beautiful in the late afternoon sun.

"It would be nice to have nothing on our minds but ourselves," Lydia said, as Quist drove up the valley and into the village of Dabney.

"Suburbia hasn't encroached here as yet," Quist said,

looking at the old white Colonial houses that lined the main street, the well-kept lawns, the flowers and shrubs. Old trees shaded the street on both sides. The air was warm but fresh. The idea of violence in such a place seemed unthinkable.

The Dabney House was something out of another time and age. It was a large, rambling building with a covered porch stretching across the front of it for the distance of a couple of city blocks. Elbow to elbow across the porch, except for the space in front of several entrances, were rocking chairs, and in the chairs, moving gently back and forth, was an army of elderly people.

"I don't think I'd better go in," Lydia said, with something like a giggle, as they pulled up by the main entrance.

"Why not?" Quist asked.

"I have on a pants suit! They'll probably turn me back at the door!"

A uniformed bellboy came down the steps to help with their luggage. He couldn't have been much under seventy years old. He gave the new arrivals a somewhat hostile look. There was nothing on the front porch to match Quist's bright yellow linen jacket or Lydia's cleverly cut mauve cotton pants suit.

"You have reservations, sir?" the old bellboy asked.

"We do," Quist said, and felt as though he ought to be helping the old man with the bags instead of the other way around.

The chairs seemed to stop rocking as if on signal. Heads turned right and left to watch the colorful parade up the steps and into the lobby. An elderly desk clerk looked worried as they approached to sign the register.

"Julian Quist and Miss Lydia Morton," Quist said.

"Ah, yes." The clerk turned to the cubbyholes filled with keys as Quist and Lydia signed the register. He turned back with keys and a letter.

"Mr. Quist is in Two A," he said to the ancient bellboy, "and Miss Morton is in Two B." He held out the letter to Quist. "This came for you in the afternoon mail, sir."

Quist frowned at the letter. It was addressed to him at Dabney House postmarked that morning from the Dabney post office. He resisted the temptation to open it. The old bellboy managed their bags up a wide, winding staircase to the second floor. He opened the doors of 2A and 2B which adjoined.

"The key to the connecting door is on your side, Miss," he said to Lydia, making it clear that virginal womanhood was being protected from God knows what horrors. He took Lydia's bags in to 2B and returned to settle Quist in 2A. It was a large, airy room with windows looking out toward the hills. The bed and the patchwork bedcover, the chairs and a small desk were handsome antiques. The only jarring note was a television set.

Quist gave the old man a generous tip. It seemed to thaw him a little. "Is there anything I can get you, sir? There is a bar on the main floor if that interests you."

"I brought some starting supplies," Quist said. "If we could have some glasses and ice."

"Right away, sir."

The minute he was alone Quist opened the envelope. There was another copy of the snapshot and a brief typewritten note.

> You have followed the first clue perfectly, Mr. Quist. Good hunting.

Quist walked over to the door that led into 2B and knocked. Lydia opened it promptly. He handed her the letter and the snapshot. She glanced at it and then up at him, her violet eyes wide.

"This was mailed here in Dabney at eleven o'clock this morning," Quist said quietly, "long before we had even thought of coming. What do you make of it?"

"I've heard of mind readers, Julian, and all the stuff that's been around about psychics. But how can someone read your mind about something you haven't thought of yet? I think I'm just a little scared."

"I'm more than a little angry," Quist said. "Somebody's playing games with us. And it looks like it's somebody here in Dabney."

Part Two

ONE

Lydia had called Walter Nichols "a thunderstorm of a man," and he turned out to be just that, changing from dark thunderclouds and jagged streaks of anger to a bland, smiling fellow of great good humor and a wry country wit. He was the owner, publisher, and editor of the *Green Mountain Journal,* which his father had founded at the turn of the century. He was a tall, big-boned man, gnarled as an old oak tree, his face a network of wrinkles, most of them produced by laughter, his eyes a piercing blue, shaded by shaggy white eyebrows that were as wildly disordered as his hair, which must have been brick red in his youth but now had only remnants of color in it. To add a kind of piratical fierceness to his appearance was a large handlebar mustache that hid strong white teeth.

Quist had called Old Nick, as Nicholas was known locally, as soon as he and Lydia were alone.

"Been waiting to hear from you," Old Nick said on the phone.

"How did you know I was coming?" Quist asked, wondering about the letter mailed that morning, before he knew he was coming.

"Called your Miss Morton to tell her the Tylers were on their way. Got your secretary. She said you were on your way here."

"My Miss Morton is with me," Quist said, liking the sound of the old man's voice.

"You want to talk," Old Nick said, "and I guess I want to talk, but not in public. Because when I talk about Abigail I expect to consume a good full quart of bourbon whiskey. How about coming to my place? I have plenty of bourbon, if you and your lady can stand it. And there's a cold ham, some store-bought potato salad, and some fresh homemade bread my housekeeper left me with fresh creamery butter to go with it. Substantial if not elegant."

"Sounds great," Quist said. "How do I find you? We're at the Dabney House."

The old man chuckled. "Fight your way through the rocking chairs, head north on Route Seven, turn left where Forty-six crosses it. Mine's the second house on the right. You can't see it, you understand. It's hidden in the woods. But there's a mailbox with my name on it. It should take you only five minutes from the time you start."

"Which will be in about ten minutes."

The house was invisible from the road. Quist and Lydia drove through woods, almost dark in the late afternoon, along a winding dirt road. And then there was a small white farmhouse in a clearing, with a blazing sunset behind it, coloring the fields and the tall mountain shapes beyond.

And there was Old Nick, shirt-sleeved, waving like a windmill for them to keep coming. If he was startled by Quist's bright colors or Lydia's pants suit he didn't show it.

"Black day," he bellowed at them as they came to a stop. "Blackest day I can remember. I've seen people die all my life, people I've known and liked, some of them violently, kids smashed up in meaningless car accidents, drownings, strokes, heart attacks. But I was never responsible. I sent Abbie down there to do something for me. My fault—what happened to her."

"Nonsense," Quist said. He opened the car door for Lydia. "This is my Miss Morton."

The old man looked her over with a kind of impertinent twinkle in his eyes. "Unfortunately, I'm too old to tell your young man to bug off and leave us to talk about the only thing men and women really talk about."

"Which is what?" Lydia asked, smiling at him.

"My father taught me longer ago than I like to remember that no matter what men and women talk to each other about the subject matter is sex. Come in. I've been holding back on that bourbon until you got here."

He took Lydia's arm and led her into the house, ignoring Quist. On the far side of the house was a wide screen porch that overlooked the incredible view. The old man guided Lydia to a high-backed wicker chair and turned to Quist, grinning.

"Forgive me, friend, but that made me feel young again for the moment. The only thing there is to go with the bourbon is the coolest, purest spring water you ever tasted. You want to spoil it with ice, that's up to you."

"We'll try it your way," Lydia said.

The old man disappeared into a kitchen that gave off the faint aroma of freshly baked bread. He came back after a moment carrying three tumblers between his rough hands, filled with a dark amber-colored liquid. It was clear the old man didn't measure his drinks. When the three of them were seated he gave Quist a cold stare.

"Do they know who did it?" he asked.

"Not yet."

Old Nick put his drink down on a side table and took a charred black pipe out of his shirt pocket and began to fill it from a red pouch of cheap tobacco. "It'll save time if I don't ask questions and you just tell me," he said.

So Quist told him, at first only the part about Abbie Tyler —her visit to the studio before David Hale's first night, the arrangement for her to have breakfast at David's apartment, the ball, the broken dress strap, the flight. Then there was the dying and the discovery by David and Peggy Hale.

"She stumbled onto a thief?" Old Nick asked. "Is that the scenario?"

"It may be the scenario you read in the papers," Quist said. "But there is more to it, quite a lot more, that is not yet for printing in the *Green Mountain Journal,* Mr. Nichols."

"Off the record? And you two can call me Nick, or anything that pleases you. The whole damn thing is so needless, so useless! I'd like to get my hands on that S.O.B.!"

"You can come right out with the words, Nick," Lydia said, smiling at the old man.

"Then I will! Sonofabitch! You know what's the matter with our world today, Miss Morton?"

"Lydia," she said.

"You know what, Lydia? We have been too long in the hands of politicians who are piously outraged by dirty words but not by dirty money! So I use the words these days. Old man's way of protesting."

Quist had taken the letter out of his pocket and he handed the snapshot of the man wearing black glasses and the blond boy to Old Nick. "Ever see this before or recognize the people?" he asked.

The old man scowled down at the snapshot. "Not sure," he muttered. "Something about it—"

"The police think it may have been taken as long as twenty-five years ago," Quist said. "That may help you place it in time."

"What's important about it?"

"Abbie was holding it in her hand when she was killed. A picture taken before she was born."

Old Nick started to put the snapshot down as though it had burned him.

"Not that picture you're holding, Nick," Quist said. "A

copy of it. Another fact while you're trying to remember. Abbie was shot with a German Luger, World War Two vintage."

"Must be thousands of those around," Old Nick said. "Half the American boys in the army brought home German souvenirs like that." He looked closer at the picture, and then he said, "Oh, Jesus!"

"You know who they are?" Quist asked, his eyes very bright.

"Sure, sure," the old man said. "Twenty-five years ago! Big deal in this village."

"Who are they?" Quist asked, fighting impatience.

The old man handed back the snapshot and looked out toward the green hills which had turned purple and the last of the sunset. "The man's name was Robert Short. The boy's name was Teddy Williams."

Quist glanced at Lydia. He wondered if she remembered the first note that had been delivered to him. "It could be called the long and the short of it." Robert Short!

"They've both been dead a long time," the old man said. "Robert Short hung himself in his jail cell in the state prison sometime along about nineteen fifty. The boy was killed in a hunting accident along with his father about six years later, right here in Dabney. First day of the deer season."

"Don't let it sit there, Nick," Quist said, sharply. "Why did Robert Short hang himself, and what was his connection to the Williams boy?"

The old man's face was bleak. "Dirty linen," he said.

"I expected that."

"And no connection whatever with Abbie Tyler! Like you said, she wasn't even born then."

"God damn it, Nick, the story, please!"

The old man looked at Lydia. "Not a story for virginal ears," he said.

"Thanks for the compliment, Nick," Lydia said, "but I'm not a virgin."

"I never thought virginity was a happy state," Nick said. "Used the word wrong. I meant ears unsullied by filth."

"The story!" Quist insisted.

The old man let his breath out in a long sigh. "It was in the winter of nineteen forty-nine," he said. "Luther Williams was the county prosecutor in those days. His boy, Teddy, went to the local high school. Luther was a big, tough, hellion of a man. He could hunt, and fish, and chop wood, and ride the hell out of a horse better than any man in town. And he was a killer as a prosecutor. More convictions in his time than ever before or since. The boy—well, he was delicate, almost girlish you might say. He couldn't compete with Luther, I suppose, so he clung to his mother's petticoats." The old man gave Lydia a wry little smile. "I don't suppose even back in nineteen forty-nine there were very many petticoats around."

"Maybe not any," Lydia said.

"Well, there was a new teacher in the school that year, Rob Short. He was an attractive, handsome fellow with a great deal of charm. Taught music and painting and poetry, I think. You didn't have to be too sophisticated to spot him for queer. I guess you call it 'gay' today. Well, Teddy Williams took all Rob Short's courses, and I guess you'd say they fell in love; a thirty-five-year-old man and a thirteen-year-old boy. Somehow it leaked. A woman teacher caught them together, I think. Luther Williams came down on the school and Rob Short like ten tons of brick."

Quist's face had turned into a cold mask. He thought he saw where this was leading, and he suddenly felt cold as night descended on the fields beyond the porch.

"The charge, I guess, was corrupting the morals of a minor," Old Nick said. "I sometimes wondered that Luther Williams didn't kill Short with his bare hands. We had a damned good high school principal in those days, a lady named Esther Moffet. She's retired now, lives down the road. She kept Luther somehow from dragging every boy in town into the picture, making a big, noisy scandal. Luther was convinced the whole school was rotten. Esther Moffet got Sam Hamner, another local lawyer, to handle the case for the school. In the end there was no public hearing, no newspaper stories, no public scandal that touched anyone but Short and young Teddy Williams."

"Wasn't Samuel Hamner the lawyer who brought up David Hale—David Halstrohm—after his parents were killed?" Lydia asked.

"He was," Nick said. "Poor Sam. He's had a couple of strokes in the last year. He's just a vegetable now."

"You mean he can't be talked to?" Quist asked.

"Oh, you can talk to him," Nick said, with a touch of bitterness, "but he won't know what you're saying, nor be able to answer you. Why?"

"Go on with the story," Quist said.

"Not much more to it," Nick said. "Short was indicted by a grand jury, tried, convicted, and sent to prison for twenty years. Teddy Williams was shipped off to school and then college. I remember he was just twenty the year he came back here to visit his family. He and Luther went deer hunting. First day of the season it was. They never came home. A search party found them in the woods. They'd both been gunned down."

"By a German Luger?"

"Hell, no, friend. It was deer season. They both got shotgun blasts in the chest. There are always accidents in deer season, people shooting at anything that moves in the bushes.

I wouldn't go hunting the first day of deer season if you offered me a drink from the Fountain of Youth and a willing blonde."

"They know who was responsible for the accident?" Quist asked.

"Nobody came forward," Nick said. "Probably nobody knew they'd done it."

"Short was dead then?"

"Five years dead. Like I told you, hung himself in his cell. Made a rope out of a bed sheet. Couldn't take it, I guess. He'd have got off in five or six years. I wonder who took that picture of him with Teddy Williams?"

"I'd give a good deal to find out," Quist said.

The old man took a tug at his pirate mustache. "What I can't figure, Julian, is what any of this could have to do with Abbie? Why would she be hanging on to that old snapshot when she was gunned down?"

Quist got up and walked to the edge of the porch. He realized he hadn't touched his drink and he carried it with him and sipped at it.

"I haven't told you the whole thing, Nick," he said, finally. He heard Lydia sigh and knew she must have been wanting him to come out with it all. "All" was the threatening letters and snapshots to Micky Grant, Gerald Laverick, and Jake Betz, the two letters with snapshots he had now received himself.

"Someone is trying to wreck David Hale's career," Quist concluded. "Someone was meant to come here to Dabney to dig up this story you've told me, Nick—and what its connection with David is. They were so sure I would come that a letter was mailed to me at Dabney House this morning, from here in town, before I'd even thought of coming, before I'd ever heard of Dabney House."

"You wouldn't stay anywhere else if you were coming to

Dabney," the old man said. He looked Quist up and down and grinned. "Anyone who knew you would know you wouldn't stay in some roadside motel and eat hamburgers."

"I have no lead at all to Abbie's involvement with the snapshot—or Rob Short and Teddy Williams," Quist said. He took a swallow of his drink. It made him feel better. "But listening to you, Nick, I have a theory. Maybe she found it somewhere and recognized it. She went to the high school. Could it have been in some old yearbook or class book? She might have recognized it as something she'd seen in Dabney without attaching any significance to it. A curiosity, to come across a Dabney picture in New York. She lets herself into David's apartment and is killed by somebody who's broken in and is robbing the place, or—" and Quist hesitated—"searching the place."

"And she's killed because she has the picture?" Lydia asked.

"She's killed because she saw the thief or searcher and could identify him later. If he was some kind of creep who broke into the apartment to steal something, anything, maybe to provide himself with money for a fix, then it had nothing to do with the snapshot. If he was someone searching David's apartment for something specific, not just some object worth stealing, then the picture may have had something to do with it."

"I don't think I'm following," the old man said, and emptied his glass.

"We know somebody is trying to destroy David," Quist said. "Maybe he was trying to find some kind of helpful evidence that could hurt David. The girl walks in on him and he shoots her because if she described him the cops would pick him up. Now, maybe he just ran after that, not knowing that she was holding that snapshot in her hand. Or, maybe something else."

Lydia's voice wasn't quite steady. "Or she never had the snapshot, never saw it. It was put in her hand by the killer after she was dead."

"To interest us," Quist said. He turned to the old man. "I think I'd like another drink, Nick."

All three of them walked into the pleasant country kitchen. The old man poured three drinks, and the spring water ran ice cold from a faucet in the sink.

"Food?" Old Nick asked.

"I suddenly don't have much appetite," Quist said. He glanced at Lydia.

"Not just now," she said.

Quist sat on the edge of the kitchen table. The white overhead light suited the harshness of his mood. "How well did you know David Hale, Nick?"

"David Halstrohm, you mean. Because that was his name when I knew him here in Dabney. In a town like this an old crock like me, a bachelor, doesn't get to know kids well, but he gets to form an opinion about a hell of a lot of them. Some of them are nice and polite to their elders and behave themselves. Some of them are noisy, arrogant jerks. David belonged to the first group, and he was a leader in school, captain of the hockey team and the baseball team, class president. That kind of boy."

"Was he involved in the Short–Williams scandal, Nick?"

The old man stared at Quist. "I'm tempted to yell at you and ask you if you're off your rocker," he said. "But I see why you have to ask the question."

"Well?"

"I can't answer that the way you'd like me to, yes or no. The records of the case were never made public. A lot of boys were questioned, and David, as one of the head ones, must have been one of them. Sam Hamner could have told you if you'd come here a year ago. Now . . . " Old Nick shrugged.

"The records would show. You see how it is, Nick. Gerald Laverick would drop David and his Night Talk show the instant he got word that David had once been involved in some homosexual scandal. He'd consider that a moral offense and a way out of his contract with David. Someone who hates David is trying to get me or the police to open up that particular can of peas."

"Someone who was here in Dabney this morning to mail that letter to you," Lydia said.

"The other letters were delivered by a messenger or messengers," Quist said. "Maybe our Judas freak had a messenger working for him here in Dabney. How do we get at the records, Nick?"

"County clerk, I suppose," the old man said. "Monday, maybe. You know, I just don't believe David was ever involved, Julian. His name may appear as one of a dozen pupils who were questioned, but not as a principal. I'd bet my next drink on that."

"Wouldn't your Miss Esther Moffet know, Nick?" Lydia asked. "The woman who was principal of the school when it happened?"

"Why didn't I think of that?" The old man poured himself a dangerously deep slug of bourbon. "Want I should call her on the phone for you?"

"Ask her if we could stop in to see her," Quist said. "Or maybe she goes to bed early."

"Esther?" the old man laughed. "Her day don't begin till after midnight. The late, late movies. She can't stand the ones they make today. Maybe she'd come over and share that fresh bread and ham with us."

"Before you call her, Nick," Quist said, "I've got one or two more questions. Did no one ever wonder if Luther Williams and his son, Teddy, had been killed on purpose?"

"I told you, it was the first day of the deer season."

"I know you told me that. But if you wanted to kill someone without too many questions being asked that would be a perfect day to try it, wouldn't it? No one would question that you were carrying a gun. You just walk away and it's called an accident."

"Why would someone have?"

"Luther Williams was a prosecutor and a tough one, you say. Someone could have held a grudge."

"Who?"

"It's your town, Nick. So, I'll ask my second question. Did Rob Short have any kind of a family?"

The old man pulled at his mustache. "Jesus!" he said. He looked steadily at Quist. "He didn't have any family here, Julian, but he had a family. He lived in a sort of rooming house at the school while he was teaching here, but there was a family somewhere. He was gay, but he had a wife somewhere and a son about Teddy's age. When the trouble exploded the defense lawyers tried to find them, but they had just vanished from anywhere they could find any trace of them."

A muscle rippled along the line of Quist's jaw. "Short's son would have been about twenty years old that deer season," he said. "Revenge had to wait till he was old enough to pull it off. But who is he, and where is he, and does he go by the name Short or has he changed it to something else? And there was a wife. Where is she and who is she?"

"I better get Esther over here," the old man said. "You've put ideas in my head I never had before."

"There's somebody around who knows," Quist said. "Somebody who wants the whole story dredged up without exposing himself. It's an uncomfortable feeling to realize I may have talked to him, whoever he is, in the last twenty-four hours."

TWO

Miss Esther Moffet, Quist decided, was quite an old doll. She had that fine-boned, aristocratic kind of face you see so often in New England. She must have been a beauty forty years ago. Her hair was white now, but she wore it pulled back from her forehead into a pony tail that was tied with a red velvet ribbon, like a young girl. Her eyes had been steeped over the years in compassion. She was wearing a brown tweed skirt and a gray cardigan. As she got out of an ancient car and came into Old Nick's house, she walked with a springy vigor for her years.

"Just about gotten up the courage to buy some of those," she said to Lydia when they were introduced.

"Some of what?" Lydia asked.

"Pants. I've still got a respectable waistline for them."

"And the right-shaped behind," Old Nick said, his eyes twinkling.

Miss Moffet gave him an affectionate look. "An irrepressible old lecher," she said. She was obviously fond of Walter Nichols.

Nick made fresh drinks and they all sat around the kitchen table. Miss Moffet's face seemed to turn hard as Quist laid out the story for her from start to finish.

"So you think Abbie's involvement in this was just an unhappy accident," Miss Moffet said when Quist was done.

"If she found the snapshot somewhere it occurred to me she might have recognized it from some old high school yearbook. Not understood its significance at the moment, just surprised to come across a picture that she knew originated in her hometown."

Miss Moffet shook her head. "The school yearbook comes out at commencement time in June. The Short–Williams thing happened in mid-winter, February. You can be sure there would have been no pictures of either of them in the yearbook. Robert Short was only at the school that one year —fall term, beginning of the winter term."

"Maybe Abbie had seen the photograph at a friend's house here in town," Lydia suggested.

"I'd say it was doubtful," Miss Moffet said. "There aren't any Williamses left in town. There never were any Shorts. No one else was apt to want to remember the old scandal."

"Nick says that Rob Short had a wife and a son," Quist said. "What do you know about them, Miss Moffet?"

Esther Moffet's eyes narrowed as she concentrated on the past. "It was the fall of nineteen forty-eight," she said. "It was my second year as principal. We'd had an art teacher for some years who'd made a home for himself at the school. He was a good, kind man, who knew how to make people appreciate."

"Something more than cow manure and sex," Old Nick said. "Peter Knowles, a good man. Had a good wife."

"In a routine medical check all the school faculty had to take at the start of the year they found he had an advanced, inoperable lung cancer," Miss Moffet said. "Nothing for it but that he should go and die somewhere, politely out of sight. He didn't want the kids to see him withering away. So I was confronted with the necessity of finding a replacement for Peter and Robert Short was among the applicants for the job. He was a shy, attractive, obviously qualified young man in his mid-thirties. I remember I had doubts about him."

"Doubts?" Quist asked.

"Just because I'm old enough to be your grandmother, Mr. Quist, doesn't mean I don't know the facts of life. I spotted Rob Short for a man with homosexual tendencies. It's not unusual to come across homosexuals of both sexes in the teaching profession. Where they're too overt I, as the head of the school, wouldn't want to risk hiring them. Not that I have any personal objection to them or their way of life. My goodness, every city and town and village in the world is full of people with homosexual tendencies. It's been made a moral issue when, in my judgment, it shouldn't have been. But I wouldn't want a teacher in my school who was trying to persuade all the students to become homosexuals, any more than I'd want one who was trying to persuade them all to become Catholics—or vegetarians, for that matter. Young people should have options in their lives, and not be pressured in the educational process to go one way or the other."

"Good girl," Old Nick said.

"So I had doubts about Rob Short," Miss Moffet said, "until he told me he was married and had a son thirteen years old. His wife, he told me, had a job in the city and the family wouldn't settle in Dabney until it was certain the job would be permanent. That sounded reasonable to me and it reassured me. So I hired him. He was so very gifted, his educational background so unusually good. But to the best of my knowledge, Mr. Quist, his wife and son never came to Dabney to visit in the few months Rob was at the school. He went to see them a few weekends. At least, that's where he said he went."

"But surely, when he was in trouble, his wife came to stand by him?"

"No-o-o, Mr. Quist, I don't believe so. Certainly not when the grand jury proceedings were in progress or later at the trial. I know that because Sam Hamner, who was legal counsel for the school, pleaded with Rob to get her to come and testify for him. You see, Sam had a theory about what had happened that no one but me would listen to."

"Oh?"

"Sam believed that young Teddy Williams was the villain of the piece, not Rob Short. Teddy was just the opposite of his father, Luther Williams. He was a very bright boy, but supersensitive and quite effeminate. It was Sam Hamner's belief that young Teddy was the seducer and not Rob Short. He'd questioned dozens of boys in the school, and not one of them reported that Rob Short had ever made any sort of pass at them or done anything suggestive. Only Teddy Williams, who had been what you might say 'caught in the act' with Rob, had anything to say. Lurid accounts of how he'd been 'led astray.' Sam believed, and I did, too, that Teddy had spotted Rob's problem and had tempted him too severely. But would any local jury believe it? Would they believe a thirteen-year-old boy could lead a grown man astray? They would not. Sam Hamner thought if Rob's wife would appear, testify that he had been living a normal life, had a son Teddy's age, that there might at least be a legal question about who corrupted who. But Rob wouldn't have it. He said no one would believe. He said his wife and boy would never get out from under the cloud. They had, Rob told us, under his own insistence, gone away, disappeared, changed their names. He threatened to say in court, if Sam persisted, that he had invented the story of their existence in order to get the job here at Dabney."

"Had he, perhaps, done just that?" Quist asked.

"No," Miss Moffet said, and her mouth closed in a straight, hard line. "Nothing would ever make me believe that. The poor man did what he thought was best for the future of his son, but in the end he couldn't take it and he hung himself. A sad story and a sad, sad man."

Quist turned his drink round and round in his long, tapering fingers. "I suggested to Nick that Rob Short's son might have come back here on the first day of the deer season, six years after the tragedy, and gotten even for his father."

"You didn't suggest any such thing!" Nick said.

"You knew damn well what I was suggesting," Quist said.

Miss Moffet looked steadily at Quist. "You're a smart young man," she said. "Would you be surprised if I told you I wondered about that the day it happened?"

"You never told me that, Esther!" Nick said. "You never told anyone that or it'd have come back to me."

"I'm a mean, old, mixed-up woman," Miss Moffet said, with a faint smile. "When I heard that Luther and Teddy Williams had been shot in the woods, I thought, to myself, that they'd got what was coming to them. I thought if I had been Rob Short's son I might have tried it."

"Then why didn't you say so?" Nick demanded.

"Because all you nice, kindly people who make up the world, Nick, would have taken off after Rob Short's son with your bloodhounds, and hung him from the nearest tree when you found him. After all, it could have been an accident, but not after you all got some other idea in your heads. I wasn't going to give anyone an idea that might justify a bloody manhunt, particularly if the man was innocent."

"Well, I'll be damned!" Old Nick said.

Quist sat in the darkness by the window in his room at the Dabney House, breathing in the sweet smells of a pure-aired summer night. He should have been asleep, but he'd found he couldn't. They'd pretty well demolished Old Nick's cold ham and potato salad, and the homemade bread with fresh creamery butter. The old man and the old woman had been extraordinary company. They could laugh, and they could think straight. They were, Quist thought, wonderfully ageless.

It had been a long, long day, having started after only a couple of hours' sleep following David Hale's party. Air, and food, and liquor, and a lovely interlude with Lydia when they'd finally gotten back to the inn, should have made for the soundest kind of sleep. But it wouldn't come for Quist. He had slipped out of bed, covering Lydia gently, slipped on his seersucker robe, and gone to the chair by the windows overlooking the town and the valley beyond. The moon made it seem like a pale daylight.

Quist knew that he was playing some kind of dangerous chess game with an unknown. You can only win at chess when you can anticipate your opponent's next move and design your own move to frustrate him. So far his opponent had led him around by the nose, anticipating exactly what he would do before he had thought of it himself. What, in the long run, was it this brilliant maneuverer wanted him to do in spite of himself? Was it as simple and obvious as it had seemed in the beginning, assistance in destroying David Hale? "The long and the short of it" that first note had said. That was an unsubtle way of making certain that when he got the snapshot and the people in it identified, when he came upon the story of Robert Short, Quist would know he was on the right track and not allow himself to be detoured.

But what would the sad story of Rob Short do to harm David Hale if it was made public? Miss Moffet, who, along with Old Nick, had promised to help Quist get to school records and court records tomorrow or Monday, had been flatly certain that David Halstrohm had been completely clean in the Short tragedy. Clean again! So how could David be hurt by it? Yet David had lied when asked about the snapshot. He had to have recognized Rob Short and Teddy Williams.

Could Abigail Tyler have been killed for no more sensible reason than to get Quist to go to Dabney? He would have come here anyway, Quist knew, because it was David's beginning place.

So he would examine records, talk to any people Old Nick and Miss Moffet thought might be helpful, get all the details about the Short case. After that the man across the chess board would tease him into his next move. What would that be? He had to figure that out or allow himself to be used to promote some kind of disaster.

There was, Quist thought, a simple answer to his dilemma. He would check out the records, talk to whoever might be helpful, and then, if Miss Moffet and Old Nick were right and David Hale was in the clear, then he could fold up his tent, go back to New York, and follow the course of minding his own business. He could stop playing someone else's game for them.

But Quist knew, deep down, that he couldn't do that just yet. Not until he could put a face to the man who was playing games with him; not until he presented David Hale with what he now knew and got an explanation for David's refusal to identify the snapshot. He couldn't live with those two mysteries unsolved.

Quist was just about to get up from his chair and return to the sleeping beauty in his bed, when his attention was caught by a lone figure coming along the deserted main street of Dabney toward the inn. It was a man, shoulders drooping as if he was suffering from an intolerable fatigue. Something held Quist, something familiar about the man. The figure turned off the sidewalk and came up the path to the front door of Dabney House. Quist got a full view of him then and recognized him. He was Gerald Laverick's stone-faced bodyguard.

Laverick had evidently kept his promise. He had turned the mice loose to find the cheese.

Early church bells woke Quist. He had finally slept in the sweet safety of Lydia's warmth. When he turned his head on the pillow he found her awake and looking at him, her deep violet eyes making no mystery of what she felt for him. With this woman belonging to you, you turned away from no challenges.

"You were up and down in the night," she said.

"How do you know? You slept like a baby."

"I don't have to wake up to know that you're gone," she said.

He reached out and touched her cheek. "Love you," he said. He propped himself up on an elbow. "Someone else has joined the party." He told her about the two-o'clock-in-the-morning arrival of Laverick's man.

"Checking out on David?"

"Laverick promised he would."

Lydia's face darkened. "It's a lovely morning, and a lovely village," she said, "but somehow I'd like to get away from here, Julian." A little shudder moved her bare shoulders. "There are too many dead men walking around alive; Robert Short and the Williamses."

"So let's get the job done."

Lydia went back to her own room to shower and dress. Quist shaved, showered, dressed, and then went to the telephone on the bedside table. He looked up Old Nick's number in the local directory and called him.

The answer was prompt, loud, and clear. "Walter Nichols here."

"It's Julian, Nick."

"You sleep well?"

"Intermittently."

"With that lady of yours, how else?" Nick said.

" 'An irrepressible old lecher' Esther called you."

"It's nice to be exposed to love now and then. I've got some not-too-happy news for you."

"Before you tell me I'd like to ask you something," Quist said. "Has anybody turned up since we left you last night to ask you to identify the snapshot?"

"No. Should someone?"

"There's a man who works for Gerald Laverick in town. I think he will."

"And what do I tell him?"

"The truth. He'll find it out one way or another. What's your bad news?"

"I talked to Ed Connors about a half an hour ago," Nick said. "He's the town clerk—the court clerk. Told him it would be a favor if you could look at the records on the Short case today, Sunday. Ed would be glad to do me a favor, but he tells me there are no records."

"Of course there are records!"

"Not any," Nick said. "It seems some newspaper man came looking for those records some time ago—maybe ten years ago. They searched for them then and they were gone. About that time they began to change the system here in town. Keeping records from over a hundred years you needed a warehouse. They transferred the old records onto microfilm. Ed's only explanation is that during that transfer time the records on the Short case got thrown away without first being photographed. He said there were two or three other cases where that happened. Careless handling."

"I wonder," Quist said. "Who was the newspaper man?"

"Ed doesn't remember a name. It's not unusual for someone to ask to see records of old court cases, real estate deals, the like. Ed only remembers this because they couldn't find the records when they looked for them."

"So we don't get to clear David through the records," Quist said, his voice hard. "We can't clear him through the lawyer for the school, Sam Hamner. A vegetable, you said. Who defended Short?"

"Hamner."

"Did Luther Williams handle the prosecution?"

"No. It wasn't thought proper in view of his kid's involvement. An assistant from the state attorney general's office prosecuted, man named Parker."

"Can we talk to him?"

"Not in this incarnation, Julian. He died some fifteen years ago. The whole story is wiped out as though it never happened."

"Not quite," Quist said. "Somebody who writes notes and sends pictures knows the whole story. How long has your friend Ed Connors been the town clerk?"

"Fifteen years—seventeen years."

"But not at the time of the Short trial?"

"No. Leroy Marvin was the town clerk in those days, but—"

"Don't tell me," Quist said. "He's dead, right?"

"Right."

Lydia had said it. Too many dead men walking around.

"Join us for breakfast, will you, Nick?"

"I'll have a cup of coffee with you. I'm a six o'clock riser. Ate long ago."

The large dining room of the Dabney House, sunlight streaming through its windows, was crowded with the rather elegant older people who seemed to make up its clientele. There was a strange kind of cathedral hush to the room. Everyone seemed to speak in the lowest of voices, the total effect sounding like a swarm of lazy bees. The click of silver against china was an almost noisy accompaniment. A white-coated waiter handed Lydia and Quist the breakfast menu. Lydia seemed to be fighting an impulse to laughter.

"If anyone were to sneeze it would sound like the atom bomb," she said, "and be just as startling." She had avoided the sensation of pants on this Sunday morning and was wearing a navy blue cotton, demurely high at the neck and long sleeved with a ruffle of lace at the wrists.

Quist leaned his golden head toward Lydia. "This isn't going to be an ideal place to talk to Old Nick. But there's something on this menu I haven't seen since I was a kid riding on a dining car. Chicken hash! Care to try it with me?"

He was writing the order for juice, hash, toast, and coffee on the slip the waiter had left him when Laverick's bodyguard appeared in the doorway and waited for the captain to take him to a table. For just a moment the man, tall, muscular, with a bony face, looked straight at Quist with pale eyes. There was no expression in them, as though he had never seen Quist before in his life.

"Don't look now," Quist said to Lydia, "but Laverick's man has just joined us."

The waiter brought them coffee and disappeared with the order slip. The captain guided Laverick's man to a single table across the room from them. Lydia watched him when he was no longer looking their way.

"I've seen him before," she said.

"So have I," Quist said. "Yesterday morning at the meeting at Laverick's. He was never a yard away from the old man, as though he expected some kind of violence."

"He's a violent man," Lydia said, frowning. "I saw him in action once."

"Where?"

Lydia sipped her coffee, looking out under her long lashes

at the man who was giving an order to his waiter. "It was about six or eight months ago. I think I mentioned it to you at the time, although it didn't have any special meaning for us. You'd flown out to Chicago to cover the Blackstone business, remember? Bobby Hilliard had tickets to see Jason Robards and Colleen Dewhurst in the O'Neill play and he invited me to go with him. Gerald Laverick was at the performance with a party of friends. During the intermission Bobby and I wandered out onto the sidewalk for a cigarette. There were a lot of kids out there shouting and yelling and waving some kind of protest signs. I don't remember what they were protesting, but it must have had something to do with Laverick Enterprises. Anyway, the old man and his party drifted out onto the sidewalk for a breath of air. One of the kids with a sign rushed up to Laverick and began shouting at him and poking his sign under the old man's nose. Then—then our friend over there appeared from somewhere. He slugged the kid, knocked his head back and forth with backhanded blows, and finally grabbed him by the throat. It—it was the most vicious, violent attack I ever saw. Bobby and two or three other men grabbed him and tried to pull him off the boy. Women were screaming, and blood was pouring out of the boy's nose and mouth. Finally some cops appeared and they dragged away—the boy! The cops and the theater management were most apologetic to Laverick. And our bully-boy over there went back into the theater and watched the rest of the play. There wasn't a mark on him. The kid had never been able to lay a finger on him."

"He was protecting his man," Quist said. "He's a bodyguard."

"He's also a sadistic killer, if you ask me," Lydia said.

"Well, anyway, he's alive," Quist said, "which is more than I can say about most of the people in Dabney I hoped to see."

"Why do you think he's here?"

"Laverick isn't satisfied with the inquiries his lawyer, Jason Crown, made about David. He's sent somebody he trusts to double-check." Quist's smile was grim. "If he has no better luck with facts than we've had, David's quite safe."

They had almost finished a delicious breakfast when Old Nick came charging in from the lobby. He refused the offer of coffee.

"But this is no place to talk," he said. "Last night after you left, Esther and I tried to make you a list of some people who might go back twenty-five years and who don't have headstones to identify them. My office is just across the street. Nobody there on Sunday. We can talk in peace."

"Fine," Quist said. "But before we go, are you friends with the management here, Nick?"

"Hotel's owned by a private corporation these days," Nick said. "I'm on the board of directors. Why?"

"Across the way there, sitting alone, man in a dark business suit? He's the one I thought might be asking you questions. He's obviously staying here. I'd like to put a name to him."

"No problem," Nick said. He beckoned the captain, who came on the double.

"Morning, Mr. Nichols."

"That man at Table Seven," Nick said.

The captain looked at a card he carried, evidently a list of table arrangements. "Malik. Joseph Malik, Mr. Nichols. He checked in last night after dinner. This is his first meal with us." And when the captain had gone: "What's interesting about him, Julian?"

"He works for Laverick Enterprises and I think he's here to dig up whatever dirt he can on David."

The old man chuckled. "He won't get very far unless he's got friends. Vermonters are closely related to clams when it comes to dealing with strangers. Dabney doesn't want to remember the Short case, so they're not likely to talk about it to an outsider."

"You talked to us," Quist said, smiling.

The old man gave his pirate's mustache a tug. "I'm a sucker for pretty women," he said, and leered happily at Lydia. "I'm also a sucker for innocent victims, like Abbie Tyler, especially when I had a hand in making her a victim. I sent her to New York."

The offices of the *Green Mountain Journal* were something out of the dark ages—an ancient press and folder, a Linotype machine that was apparently held together with baling wire, the pungent odor of printer's ink, and a wild scattering of clippings, notes, papers. Old Nick cleared off a couple of wooden kitchen chairs for Quist and Lydia, and sat down at his wildly disordered desk with a broad grin on his face.

"Secret of my success," he said. "Nobody can find anything in this place but me." He reached into the inside pocket of his black alpaca jacket for an envelope. There were some names scribbled on the back of it. "Going back twenty-five years turns out to be a gloomy business, Julian. As you've learned already, most of the key people are either dead or non comp. Esther remembers there were about a dozen boys in the school questioned by authorities in addition to Teddy Williams. David Halstrohm was one of them, of course. Five others have got their names on a tablet on the village green. Killed in wars. Two in a plane crash in Europe, NATO forces. One in Korea. Two in Vietnam. You suppose that's a national average of what's happened to American youth over the last quarter century?"

"An ugly figure," Quist said.

"That leaves six who should be alive and kicking," Nick said. "But you have to know that young people don't hang around small towns like Dabney anymore. No future, no jobs, no opportunities. Would you believe not one of those six is still living here in town?"

"Their families?"

"Thinned out," Nick said. "Some of them dead, some of them moved away and forgotten." He glanced at his list. "The Harwoods, dead. The Wests, dead. George Hazleton is still around, but his wife is dead. The Walbergs sold their dairy farm right after the case and moved away, God knows where. The Bennetts are living with—"

"Hold it!" Quist said. "The Walbergs?"

"They had a dairy farm down in the valley. Sold the whole kit and caboodle the year of the Short case and moved away."

"Their son named George? A fat boy?" Quist asked.

Nick frowned. "I don't remember the boy, nor the Walbergs much either. Not very social, I guess."

Quist glanced at Lydia. "There's a man named George Walberg, Pudge to his friends, who works for David. He must have recognized that snapshot but he never said so."

"Do we know that he ever saw it?" Lydia asked.

It was possible he hadn't, but the faithful Pudge could certainly be a source of information.

Nick didn't seem to see the importance of this and he finished his list. "As I was saying, the Bennetts are living with a daughter in Manchester. Finally, there are the Coles. The senior Coles are in the cemetery, but Pete Cole, the brother of Jerry Cole who was questioned, runs a garage here in town."

Quist was restless. David and Pudge Walberg were going to have to come clean. Was there any point in wasting time on the people who were left here in Dabney?

"Esther reminded me of one thing. These boys weren't questioned in a group, Julian. Each one was questioned separately. No one of them would know what any other of them had to say, unless they talked to each other afterwards."

Quist's attention had drifted. He was thinking about a hunting accident. "I'd like to get a lead to Rob Short's family if I could—wife and son. Miss Moffet hired him when she was principal. You suppose there are some records somewhere that would tell us what Short's home address was when he applied, where the wife worked? Miss Moffat said she had a job in the city. I suppose that means New York."

"Only place we ever call 'the city,' " Nick said. He reached for the phone on his desk and dialed a number. He must have let it ring eight or ten times before he put down the receiver. "Esther's probably working out in her garden. She won't admit she's a little deaf."

"Could we drive over and talk to her? I'd like to ask her about Pudge Walberg, too."

"Why not?"

Esther Moffet lived in a little saltbox cottage not too far from Old Nick's place. On the outside it was a model of loving care—neatly cut lawn, flowerbeds cultivated and edged, shrubs trimmed and clipped. At the back was a fenced-in garden that was a place of magic colors.

"Esther!" Old Nick shouted, as he headed for the back door.

The old man knocked loudly, and when there was no answer, he walked in like a member of the family. He'd only taken a step or two into the cottage when Quist and Lydia heard him cry out.

"Jesus God!"

The kitchen, which must ordinarily have been a dream of orderly perfection, was a mess. Pots and pans had been scattered about. Closets had been opened and packages of food staples thrown around. China had been taken out of glassed-in cupboards and dropped on the floor, much of it smashed.

"Esther!" Old Nick shouted, his voice now hoarse with anxiety.

He stumbled over an iron saucepan as he barged into the living room. More disaster. Books scattered out of the bookcases, cushions ripped out of chairs and cut open, the stuffing spread around, a once neat desk taken apart. And at the foot of the stairs leading to the second floor lay Miss Moffat. Nick was frozen by the sight of her. It was Quist who went quickly to her and knelt beside her.

Miss Moffet was wearing a blue woolen robe over a plain white nightgown. Both garments were spattered with blood. She had been subjected to a terrible beating. Her face looked lopsided, a broken jaw, Quist guessed. Her closed eyes were swollen and discolored. Quist's fingers touched her throat for some sign of a pulse.

"Get an ambulance here, Nick," he said, in a cold, hard voice. "She's still alive. Not much life, but alive."

Old Nick seemed unable to move and it was Lydia who made the call. Quist stepped across the body and ran up the stairway to the second floor. The upstairs had been subjected to the same violent search. He found a quilted bedcover and a pillow and brought them downstairs. He lifted the old woman's head and she made a small sound, and her blue lips were flecked with a red, bubbling foam. He put the pillow under her head and covered her with a quilt.

"She's cold as ice," he said. "Where's the hospital, Nick?"

"Bennington," Old Nick muttered. "Nearly forty miles."

"Better have a doctor here before she's moved."

"Oh, God, please tell me who did this!" Old Nick said.

"Joseph Malik," Lydia whispered.

Quist stood up. "Sonofabitch!" he said. "You two stay with her. Try to have a doctor see her before some volunteer ambulance people move her. But if you can't get a doctor here at once let them take her. She needs help just as quickly as she can get it."

"I'm going with you!" Old Nick said.

"You stay here!" Quist said, his voice shaken. "They'll ask Lydia, a stranger, a thousand questions. Go with her to wherever they take her. I'll find you. If she ever gets to speak it may be vital she has a friend to speak to."

"Julian!" Lydia called out as he headed for the kitchen. He turned back. "He's a killer. I told you. A sadistic killer. Please be careful!"

Quist laughed. His mood was not careful.

THREE

Quist drove along the winding dirt road, faster than the loose gravel made sensible, the rear end of the rented car swinging like a tail in the wind.

Why? Why Esther Moffet? What could she possibly have that Malik wanted so badly—if it was Malik? Laverick had sent him here to check out on David Hale. It was a double-check on David, who had already been investigated by Jason Crown, the lawyer. Why in God's name the violence? Suppose Malik had got someone who'd identified the snapshot? It might well have taken him to Miss Moffet, principal of the school when the Short scandal had erupted. But why the terrible beating? Why the search and for what? Malik—or whoever—had expected to find something—something that could be hidden in a china closet or a bookcase or a bureau drawer. "Smaller than a breadbox" as they used to say on "Twenty Questions."

He swung out onto the main highway. The Dabney House was a mile and a half away.

Quist found himself toying with and rejecting a line of thought he'd had yesterday in David Hale's apartment. Abbie Tyler could have been killed by a casual thief, a housebreaker unconnected with anything connected to David's life. The snapshot gripped in Abbie's hand had made him doubt.

Not for a second could you believe "casual thief" about Miss Moffet's disaster. She had not been just knocked out, she'd been worked over. To make her talk? And no casual thief would tear a house apart the way Miss Moffet's cottage had been demolished. This man was looking for something specific, something he didn't expect to find anywhere else except in Miss Moffet's possession.

Quist brought his car to a skidding stop in the parking lot of the Dabney House. Heads in the rocking chairs turned as he ran up the front steps and into the lobby. The room clerk looked startled. Quist's face was white with anger.

"Mr. Joseph Malik. His room number, please," Quist said.

The clerk turned away toward the cubbyholes and then back again. "I believe Mr. Malik checked out a little while ago, sir. Right after breakfast."

While they sat talking in Old Nick's office.

Quist turned around and spotted the ancient bell man who had dealt with them on their arrival. He went over to him. "Did you see Mr. Malik check out?" he asked.

"Don't know as I know a Mr. Malik, sir."

Quist described Laverick's man. Then he remembered Table 7. Could that correspond to Room 7? He suggested it.

"It's against house policy for us to talk about the guests, sir."

"I don't have much time to argue with you," Quist said. He reached in his pocket and brought out some folding money held in a silver clip. He detached a ten-dollar bill. "My card," he said. "My name is Alexander Hamilton."

The old man moistened his lips, glanced at the desk, and snatched away the bill, as if he were stealing it. "I think Mr. Malik left directly after breakfast, sir. I carried his bag to his car for him."

"His car, or was it a local rental like mine?"

"His car I would think, sir. New York license."

"You didn't happen to take notice of the license, did you?"

"Well—as a matter of fact I did, sir. Only because it was

an odd one. No numbers, just letters. LVCK."

Laverick! Laverick would have a personalized number plate.

"What kind of car was it?"

"It was a gray Mercedes-Benz, sir."

"Where is the local state police barracks?"

"In Rutland, sir. There's a resident trooper here in Dabney. Name of Spofford."

"If I catch up with Mr. Malik I might just introduce you to Andrew Jackson," Quist said.

"I'm afraid you won't catch him, sir. He's got an hour's start on you."

"There are still telephones," Quist said.

He went to a booth in the corner of the lobby, asked for the resident trooper's number, and was connected with a woman. Trooper Spofford wasn't at home. Where could he be found? It was urgent.

"He just took off for Miss Esther Moffet's place. You know where that is?"

"I know where that is," Quist said.

He called Miss Moffet's number and it was Lydia who answered.

"Our friend has flown the coop," he said. "You got help yet?"

"The ambulance has just come, Julian."

"Doctor?"

"On his way. He should be here any minute. The boys on the ambulance want to wait for him. She's pretty badly off."

"There's a state trooper headed your way. When he gets there—"

"He's just driving in the yard, Julian."

"Let me talk to him."

The wait seemed intolerable. Finally Trooper Spofford identified himself.

"You haven't had time, I know, to get oriented," Quist said. "But I think I may know who attacked Miss Moffet. He's a man named Malik and he's been on the road to New York for about an hour in a gray Mercedes-Benz, license LVCK."

"What have you got on him?" Spofford asked.

"Too long a story. I'll be out there in ten minutes. But if the cops could pick him up and go through his luggage you may find some bloody clothes. He couldn't have done that job on Miss Moffet without getting some of her blood on him."

"If he went down Route Seven he should be past Williamstown by now," Spofford said. "We can't hold him without a charge."

"You search people for drugs, don't you? You may not find any drugs on him, but if they find any bloody clothes in his bag, you've got him on a criminal assault charge. Let's hope it's no worse than that."

"Let's hope not," Spofford said. "Miss Moffet was my English teacher a long time ago. I wouldn't like it for her not to pull through."

Quist drove back toward Miss Moffet's cottage. Just before he came to the dirt drive the ambulance appeared, top lights blinking, siren beginning to howl. Quist pulled to one side to let it pass. He got a glimpse of Old Nick bending over the patient on a stretcher.

Lydia was standing in the back garden when he drove in. She came to him quickly, and for a moment he held her trembling body in his arms.

"They don't think she's got much chance," she whispered.

Quist had noticed the trooper's car and another at the front of the house.

"Doctor?"

"He's riding the ambulance with her and Nick," Lydia

said. "Everybody loves that old gal, Julian. The doctor, the ambulance boys, the trooper—all went to her school, all touched by her in some fashion. The doctor, a youngish man, had tears running down his cheeks, unashamed, when he got through examining her. If you'd produced your Joseph Malik, there might have been a lynching on the main street of Dabney."

"If it was Malik."

"Do you have any doubts, Julian?"

"There's not a shred of proof and the violence doesn't make sense for a professional." Quist bent down and kissed Lydia's cheek. "Let's hope they pick him up. Some bloody clothes would sew it up tight."

Trooper Spofford was a trim, tanned young man in his late twenties, his eyes hidden by tinted glasses. He was standing in the middle of Miss Moffet's wrecked kitchen.

"Never saw anything like this in my life," he said, after Quist had introduced himself. "Special squad is on its way from Rutland. That bastard must have left his fingerprints on a hundred different objects in this house. Seems like there wasn't anything left untouched."

"Maybe," Quist said. The tinted glasses turned his way. "If it's the man I think it was, Trooper, he didn't leave his fingerprints on anything. He's a professional. You had a chance to put out an alarm on him?"

Spofford nodded. "They should pick him up around Pittsfield, Massachusetts, I'd guess. If he sticks to the main roads, of course."

"Or if he didn't head for Albany or some other direction," Quist said.

"I got a little information from Mr. Nichols and Miss Morton," Spofford said. He glanced at Lydia who was standing in the doorway. "I understand you came up here last evening to ask some questions about David Hale and Abbie Tyler."

Quist sketched it out for him. Muscles knotted along the trooper's jaw as he listened.

"Abbie was one of the nicest girls in this town," Spofford said. "And Miss Moffet—all I can tell you is she's a great lady. Isn't a kid grew up in this town going back thirty-five years didn't have something good rub off her. Two nice people. Why, Mr. Quist?"

"I don't know—yet. But it all goes back to the Short case and some connection David Hale had with it."

"What does Hale say it is?"

"He hasn't said. I haven't had the right questions to ask him until now. Look, Miss Morton and I would like to go on to the hospital. If there's any chance Miss Moffet can identify the man who did this, and if he was Joseph Malik, I want him picked up on the other end. The homicide man in charge of the Tyler murder is a friend of mine and I have a hunch—pure hunch, not evidence—that Malik is the man he wants, too. I'll call you from the hospital, unless you have some objection to our going."

"I guess it's okay," Spofford said. "Mr. Nichols vouches for you both."

"And I've got a little side mystery you might help me solve," Quist said. He took the letter with the snapshot in it out of his pocket. "This was waiting for me when we checked in at the Dabney House last evening, Spofford. It was mailed in Dabney at eleven o'clock yesterday morning. At eleven o'clock yesterday morning I had no idea I was coming to Dabney, and I'd never heard of the Dabney House. Someone in this town was way ahead of me. The picture, by the way, is one taken a good twenty-five years ago and copied recently. The man is Robert Short, who hung himself in a jail cell, and the boy is Teddy Williams, who was killed in a hunting accident along with his father some six years after that. They were the principals in a homosexual scandal at the school." Quist shook his head. "How in the world you can find out who mailed this to me I don't know, but it might shine a lot of light on things if you could."

Quist and Lydia drove to the Dabney House, packed their things, and checked out. Quist wanted to be able to move back to New York without any holdups when the moment came. They drove down a long, lovely green valley toward Bennington and the hospital. Lydia sat close to Quist, her shoulder against his. The unreal violence of the last twenty-four hours called for the reassurance of his nearness. She was wearing dark glasses to protect her eyes from the bright sun.

"You suggested to Spofford that Malik might be responsible for Abbie," she said, after they'd driven for some time in silence.

"I told him hunch, not any kind of evidence," Quist said. "Someone was searching for something in David's apartment when Abbie interrupted him. The next night someone was searching for something in Miss Moffet's cottage and a violence took place. They're look-alikes, luv. And there is the further link that Abbie and Miss Moffet and David are all from Dabney. And that the person who's playing games with us with letters and snapshots is concerned with Dabney's history." He lifted his right hand and brought it down hard on the wheel. "I'm beginning to develop a notion, Lydia, that we're dealing with two people or sets of people. One of them is the letter writer, the picture sender, who wants us to find out something. They've laid a trail for us, carefully, that brought us to Dabney. Then there is a second set who will go to any lengths to keep us from finding out what the first set wants. We're being used by the first set, and we're apt to get our heads blown off by the second set if we get too close to whatever it is we're supposed to find."

"How about a summer vacation in the south of France?" Lydia asked.

"Malik is Laverick's man," Quist said, ignoring the question. "Laverick wants to protect a multimillion-dollar investment in Night Talk. If there's some dirt on David that would blow it he wants to be able to get out of the deal. He doesn't want to protect David, he just wants the truth. Why would he send Malik out on a killing spree? Laverick Enterprises is more powerful than whole governments! Why kill a kid reporter and a retired old lady, harmless, gentle people? Malik seemed so obvious in the first shock of seeing Miss Moffet, but I begin to wonder. There are other people who have a great deal more to lose than Laverick—careers, economic futures. Laverick has such great power he wouldn't have to protect himself with this kind of hysterical bloodletting."

"Unless your letter writer got everybody moving too fast," Lydia suggested.

"One of the people who was supposed to get moving was Laverick himself. He got a letter, remember."

"I still say the south of France is a great idea," Lydia said.

Quist reached out and touched her knee. "I'll buy it, but not until we've squared accounts for Abbie and Esther." He slowed down to make the turn into the drive leading up to the hospital. "It's quite possible, you know, that Abbie wasn't our killer's first murder victim. There was that alleged hunting accident nineteen years ago that wiped out a father and son, connected to David, connected to Pudge Walberg, connected to Esther Moffet, and, since she was hanging onto that snapshot and since she came from Dabney, perhaps connected to Abbie Tyler."

"Who wasn't born when they were killed." Lydia shook her head. "I'll still say Malik. I saw him work once, and Miss Moffet and her cottage looked like his kind of ball game."

The hospital was white and clean and cold. People moved briskly as though they were in a perpetual hurry. Inquiry at the main desk sent Quist and Lydia to a third floor waiting room where they found Old Nick, slumped in an aluminum-backed chair, looking shriveled and exhausted. His enormous energy seemed to have drained away.

"You find your man?" he asked.

"Took off before I could," Quist said. "We'll pick him up. How are things here?"

"Bad, I'm afraid. Real bad. Broken jaw, probable skull fracture, broken ribs, probable internal injuries. One eye may not work again, if anything works again. God damn, God damn, God damn!" The old man's voice choked in his throat.

"No chance she can talk?" Quist asked.

"Not now. Maybe never."

A white starched nurse came up to them. "Mr. Quist? State Police Trooper Spofford wants to talk to you on the phone. You can take it over there."

Quist went over to a wall phone and answered.

"We picked up your man in Stockbridge, Mass.," Spofford said. "Nothing to hold him on. No bloodstained clothes. He was traveling light. Just a clean shirt and a shaving kit in his bag. No blood stains on the clothes he was wearing—a charcoal gray business suit."

Quist felt his muscles tighten. "I saw him twice in Dabney, Spofford. The first time was about two o'clock this morning. I saw him come into the hotel and he was wearing tan slacks and a corduroy jacket. The second time was at breakfast this morning and he was wearing that charcoal gray suit. Just as sure as God that corduroy jacket and those tan slacks have been tossed into the woods, maybe buried somewhere, between Dabney and Stockbridge."

"Quite a piece of territory to search," Spofford said. "They had nothing they could hold him on, Mr. Quist. Operator's license okay, car registration okay."

"Maybe some kid will find the clothes in the woods somewhere. I'm convinced all over again, Spofford, that Malik's our man."

Quist turned back to Lydia and Nick and saw that they'd been joined by a doctor in a green operating suit. He was the Dabney man who'd ridden the ambulance down with Miss Moffet, the young man who had shed a tear for her.

"This is Doc Sherrill, Julian," Old Nick said.

The doctor shook his head. "It's hard to believe the fury of the attack," he said. "Any one of a dozen blows must have knocked Miss Esther cold. You'd have to believe this man went on beating and beating her after she was unconscious."

"Her chances?"

"One in ten," the doctor said. "Knowing it was a police case they took special precautions in cleaning her up. They thought she might have clawed at her attacker, might be flesh or particles of hair under her fingernails. What they found was a few nylon threads. That's all. Made us wonder whether she might have been beaten by a woman and had managed to grab at her stockings."

Quist shook his head. His mouth was a straight, hard slit. "The most stylish thing for criminals today is the stocking mask," he said. "I'm afraid those nylon threads under Miss Moffet's fingernails simply mean that if she does regain consciousness and can talk she won't be able to give us a description of the man."

Quist made a collect call from the hospital's business office to Lieutenant Kreevich in New York. He finally traced the homicide man to his own apartment in Manhattan.

"You have to get a change of clothes and wash behind your ears once in a while," Kreevich said. "Did Dabney produce any results?"

Quist told his story slowly and in detail. Kreevich didn't interrupt except for a muttered four-letter word here and there.

"Your Miss Moffet won't be able to talk?" Kreevich asked when Quist had come to the end.

"Not in the foreseeable future."

"No question it was Malik you saw coming into the hotel up there in the middle of the night? I mean, how good was the light? Could you have been mistaken?"

"No way. I saw him coming into the hotel, recognized him. I'd seen him that morning in Laverick's office."

"And you saw him wearing at least two sets of clothes?"

"I saw. He should be tooling into the city sometime in the next hour. I haven't got anything on him except my personal conviction, Mark, but I sure as hell wouldn't want him to skip town on us."

"If you can swear he was in Dabney this morning . . ."

"Hell, he was registered at the inn under his own name, driving a car in Laverick's."

"Okay," Kreevich said. "But now I have to move in on Hale and his friend Walberg."

"I'd like it if you could wait for me," Quist said. "To you the people involved are just names on a police report. To me they're flesh and blood and I care for one or two of them. More than that, I know more about the background up here than you do. I can ask better questions."

"How long will it take you to get back here?"

"Lydia's trying to charter us a plane from here in Bennington. Say, two hours. Can you have David and Walberg in my apartment then? They may talk a little easier there than at police headquarters."

"Two hours," Kreevich said.

Quist then made another collect call to Dan Garvey. Once more he sketched out the whole story. "I'm interested in something that dates way back, Dan. I want to locate Robert Short's wife and son. According to Walter Nichols and Miss Moffet, the wife had a job in New York at the time of the scandal. That means she must have had a Social Security number and an address of some sort."

"Today is Sunday," Garvey said. "How the hell do I dig up Social Security information?"

"Work a miracle," Quist said. "We must know someone. Be at my apartment in two hours, and you might try to locate Connie and ask her to be there too."

"I doubt the miracle," Garvey said, "but I'll try."

When he rejoined Lydia, Quist learned that she had done it. A young man in Bennington had agreed to fly them to New York. Dr. Sherrill would drive their rented car back to Dabney. He had other patients he had to cover.

"It's going to be a long haul for Miss Moffet if she makes it at all," the doctor said.

"I'll keep in touch with you and Nick," Quist said. He turned to Old Nick, whose mustache seemed to have drooped with his spirits. "The best thing you can do for me, Nick, is to try to find out who mailed that letter to me in Dabney yesterday morning."

"Needles in haystacks don't reveal me at my best," the old man said. "I don't quite know how to go about it, but we'll see." He raised his red-rimmed eyes to Quist. "What you can do for me is let me know when you've got that man Malik nailed to the cross. Because if you don't manage it soon, Julian, I may take care of it myself—if Esther doesn't make it!"

The flight to New York in a Piper Cub was uneventful. They taxied in to the city from the airport. They walked into the lobby of Quist's Beekman Place apartment building twenty minutes ahead of their promised two hours.

"Letter for you, Mr. Quist, delivered by messenger," the

doorman said, and handed over the now familiar plain white envelope with Quist's name typed on the face of it.

Quist's hands weren't quite steady as he opened it. That sonofabitch across the chess board was ahead of him again, as he had been from the beginning.

> Well done so far, Mr. Quist [the note read]. The next questions you should ask are (1) What was Robert Short's real name? (2) Who would commit murder rather than have his connection with Robert Short revealed? (3) Could it be your straw man, David Hale, or could it be someone you haven't dreamed of?

Quist handed the note to Lydia and his lips moved in a silent profanity.

Quist had just finished pouring himself a Jack Daniels on the rocks at the bar in the corner of his sunny living room when the front doorbell rang. Lydia had gone up to the second floor of the duplex to shower and change. Quist took a swallow of his drink and drew a deep breath. He didn't relish facing the next move in the game. Kreevich had arrived at exactly two hours to the minute.

The detective stood outside the door with David and Peggy Hale and a sweating Pudge Walberg. There were muttered hellos as they came into the living room. The Hales knew the apartment well. Walberg looked around at the modern furniture, the modern paintings on the walls, the French doors opening out onto a terrace that overlooked the East River. He looked like a man in a trap who was searching for a way out.

"I insisted on bringing Peg with me," David said, his resonant voice quite steady. "She knows everything there is to know now. The lieutenant has told me about Miss Moffet.

Is there any fresh news of her?"

"She has an outside chance," Quist said.

"Jesus!" David said. "Well, where do you want to begin, Julian? Oh, yes, I recognized the people in the snapshot—Rob Short and Teddy Williams. But I want you to know that Peg didn't. She'd never seen them, of course." He looked down at his wife who was holding on to his arm. They were in it together, whatever it was. "I'd had no chance to talk to Peg at the party when the snapshots first showed up. We were never alone. On the way home I was trying to figure out what to do, but I planned to tell her when we were in our apartment. Of course, when we got there we found the Tyler girl."

"I knew about the scandal," Peggy Hale said. "David and I had just been married—for the first time—when the hunting accident that killed Teddy Williams and his father took place. That was when David told me. David wondered at the time if it really was an accident, but after the inquiry was over and the matter settled, I don't think we ever talked about it again until yesterday."

Lydia came down the spiral staircase from the second floor at that moment wearing a pale yellow housecoat. She walked over to Peggy Hale and kissed her cheek. "I don't imagine this is going to be a short session," she said. "Are you all just going to stand here? Won't you sit down? I'll make you drinks, or coffee, or whatever you want."

The Hales sat together on the couch. Pudge Walberg wandered over to the French doors, as if he were contemplating a jump off the terrace. Kreevich, grim but silent, took a chair near the bookcases and lit a cigarette. He was willing to let this be Quist's party for a while, at least. Coffee seemed to be the order of the day, and Lydia disappeared into the kitchenette.

"You weren't concerned about David's involvement with

Robert Short?" Quist asked Peggy.

She laughed and looked up at David's dark, handsome face. "You mean did I wonder if David might be queer? I was married to him. I knew damn well he wasn't queer, Julian."

"The court records will show that I had no direct connection with Rob Short," David said. "Did you get a look at them in Dabney?"

"There are no court records," Quist said.

"But of course there are!"

"There are no court records, David. There haven't been any for at least ten years." Quist explained about the microfilm slipup. "Either that's the explanation or somebody got to them and destroyed them long ago. Would those records have involved you, David? I never did get the whole story from Walter Nichols and Miss Moffet. I don't think either of them knew the whole story. And the lawyer for Short, who later turned out to be your guardian, isn't able to talk."

"Poor Uncle Sam," David said. "He would so much rather be dead."

"Who is Uncle Sam?" Kreevich asked.

"Samuel Hamner," David said. "He was a local lawyer who defended Short and, you might say, the school. My parents were killed about a year after the scandal in a railroad-crossing accident, and Sam Hamner became my legal guardian. He was an old friend of my father's and the family lawyer. He's had a couple of strokes and he—he just sits there."

"Suppose, David, you tell us the Robert Short story right from the start," Quist said.

David gave his wife's hand a reassuring pat and then he got up and began to prowl around the room. "I was a sophomore in school," he said. "There was a man named Knowles, a great old guy, who had taught art and poetry classes in the school forever. He got seriously sick just before the school year began in the fall of forty-eight and Miss Moffet came up with a replacement for him, a man named Rob Short. He was an unusual man; not the ordinary teacher type. He asked the kids in his classes to call him 'Rob' when it wasn't a formal function. None of the other teachers did that. I suppose he was in his mid-thirties. You might have called him handsome, except that he looked worn and a little seedy. Leather patches at his elbows, not because it was the thing to do in those days, but because his clothes were old and—and needed help." David paused to accept a mug of coffee from Lydia. Nobody broke the moment of silence.

"He wasn't really a good teacher," David went on, "in the routine way. I remember catching him looking in the back of the book for the answers to questions in an art history class. But for a few of us he was unforgettable. He was a good painter, loved classical music, and he could spout poetry by the yard. If you were interested, he could set you on fire with his own enthusiasm. But somehow I don't think he had any formal training as a teacher. Miss Moffet would know that from his record when he applied for the job."

"I hope for her sake she can tell us anything," Quist said.

"I had just the one class with him, art history," David said. "I was sports happy. I played football and hockey and baseball in season. I knew that Mr. Short gave extra time, free time, to kids who were interested in the arts." He hesitated again. "I'm not sure I should be the one to tell you the next part of this." His dark eyes were focused across the room on Pudge Walberg.

Walberg turned as though it was a cue he'd been expecting. He mopped at his perspiring face with an already damp handkerchief. "Rob Short was a good, kind, man; a man with sympathy and compassion," Walberg said, his voice husky. "I was twelve years old and one of half a dozen kids who boarded at the school. I was sent to stay there because there was no school bus route anywhere near my family's farm. There was an old house next to the school where the boarders stayed, and Mr. Short was placed in charge. A local woman came in to prepare our meals for us, a Mrs. Avery. I was miserable, homesick, unhappy. I was a fat boy, the butt of jokes, no good at sports. Rob Short understood, and he'd take time to comfort me, to read aloud to me, to let me listen to music with him on his record player. That was all. Nothing else." Walberg paused to gulp in some air. Lydia carried the coffeepot over to him and his cup rattled as he held it for her.

"Just after the Christmas holidays," Walberg said, "Teddy Williams came to stay at the school for a few days. He was a beautiful kid with blond curly hair, attractive in an arrogant sort of way. Of course, he was a day scholar regularly and he took courses with Mr. Short, and I thought he was a little bit of a favorite with Mr. Short. One evening I was having a problem with some homework. Math, as I remember it. I went looking for Mr. Short, but I couldn't find him. Then I remembered that Teddy Williams was a whiz at math and went to his room to find him. I—I just walked in, and I had the hell scared out of me. I—I was too unsophisticated in those days to guess what was going on, but somehow I knew I shouldn't be there, and that whatever was going on was wrong.

"I got the hell out of there and started to run down the hall to my room. Before I got there I came face to face with Mrs. Avery. She asked if I knew where Mr. Short was, and I was so confused and bewildered I said something about his being in Teddy's room. I got to my room and got the door closed when all hell broke loose down the hall, Mrs. Avery screaming and yelling, and Mr. Short pleading with her. I remember I covered my head with my bed pillow because I couldn't bear the sound of it." Walberg struggled for breath for a moment. "A while later the door to my room opened and I looked out from under the pillow and there was Mr. Short. He was white as paper. I thought I never saw a man who looked so sad.

" 'Did you have to tell Mrs. Avery where I was, Georgie?' he asked me. 'Oh, God, boy, do you know what you've done to me? Do you have any idea?'

"A little while later the state police came along with Teddy's father and they took Mr. Short away. And then Miss Moffet came into my room and asked me questions I really didn't understand. Eventually I cried myself to sleep because I felt I'd betrayed Mr. Short, who was one of the only friends I had. You know what I think today?"

"I'd like to know," Quist said, quite gently.

"I think Mr. Short had a problem he was fighting with all his might. I think he was okay until Teddy Williams came into the picture. I think Teddy was an old hand at that kind of thing. I think he broke down Mr. Short's resistance—seduced him, you might say."

Walberg turned away toward the terrace.

"Did Short ever mention a wife and a son to you, Pudge?" Quist asked.

"Once I remember he said he had a boy about my age. That was all. Never anything about his wife; never anything more than that about his son."

"To you, David?" Quist asked.

"Never," David said. "But I heard something to that effect from Sam Hamner during the investigation by the grand jury and afterwards. Uncle Sam wanted the wife and child to come forward, stand by Mr. Short. But he refused to involve them. He wouldn't even say where they were or how they could be found. And they never came forward of their own accord."

"So we come to your involvement in it, David."

"I wasn't 'involved' in any real sense," David said. "The special prosecutor they brought in and Uncle Sam Hamner, in turn, questioned most of the boys who had taken any classes with Mr. Short. We were questioned separately but I imagine we were all asked the same question. Bluntly, had Mr. Short ever made a pass at us. He'd certainly never even put a hand on me. I may have heard more talk about it than the other kids because Uncle Sam was in and out of our house, and he trusted me not to spill anything I heard talked about."

"And what did you hear talked about?"

"Only that there was no evidence that there'd ever been anyone but Teddy Williams. Luther Williams, Teddy's father, kept insisting that his son was only one part of a sort of mass corruption. I guess that was because he was ashamed of Teddy."

"You testified before the grand jury?" Quist asked.

"Along with some others, including Pudge. I guess we all said Mr. Short was in the clear as far as we were concerned. But Mrs. Avery was all they needed to bring in an indictment and all the prosecutor needed to get a conviction at the trial. The poor devil hung himself when he'd only been in jail a few months."

"So there's nothing Laverick could pin on you, or that could do you any public damage?" Kreevich asked, breaking his silence.

"Nothing."

"Then why did you refuse to identify the picture? Why did you stall and lie?"

"I needed time to think, Lieutenant," David said. "The letters people got seemed to be attacking me. If I identified the snapshot when I first saw it at the party we'd have had a city full of conclusion jumpers. It doesn't take much to wreck a reputation in this business. I was puzzled. Who was out to get me? Who could know of my fringe connection to the Short case twenty-five years ago? How did they propose to use it? My first impulse was just to lie low because the truth couldn't hurt me. It was a mistake, I suppose, but what harm has it done?"

Kreevich bounced up out of his chair. "I don't know what harm it's done, Mr. Hale, but we have a dead girl and a nearly dead woman who had 'fringe connections' to the Short case. Your silence kept us from having any direction for a day and a half until Julian dug out some of the truth."

"One more thing," Quist said. He took the latest letter out of his pocket. "I've now had three of these from our threatening friend, David. In this one he says I should be asking some questions. First, what was Robert Short's real name?"

David stared at him, blankly. Kreevich came around to look over Quist's shoulder at the note.

"Was any other name ever mentioned at the time, David? Did Sam Hamner ever tell you that 'Short' wasn't the man's name?"

"Never."

"Second: Who would commit murder rather than have his connection with Robert Short revealed? He then goes on to speculate on whether or not it might be you, David."

"But I—"

"You didn't kill Abbie Tyler," Quist said. "We know that. Do we know that you weren't in Dabney last night beating up Miss Moffet?"

"We know that," Kreevich said. "While I knew Mr. Hale wasn't telling me all he knew, I made sure he didn't run out of town on me."

"Robert Short's real name," Quist said. "You don't recall anything to suggest that this man was teaching at your school under an alias?"

"Nothing."

"Because it would be helpful in finding his wife and son if their name isn't Short."

"I never heard it suggested or even hinted at," David said. "You, Pudge?"

Walberg turned back from the terrace. " 'Robert Short' is all I ever heard," he said.

Quist remembered the first note—"the long and the short of it." Well, they knew what "the short of it" was now. But the "long" of it? This letter-writing bastard had them going in circles, which was probably exactly what he wanted.

"Until just now I hadn't connected you with the Dabney contingent, Mr. Walberg," Kreevich said. "Did you know Abbie Tyler or her parents?"

Pudge Walberg shook his head. "My family had a dairy farm near Dabney. That's where I grew up. But they sold the farm and moved away the year after the thing with Mr. Short."

"Any connection?"

"With Mr. Short? Oh, no. Small farms were getting harder and harder to keep going, even back then," Pudge said. "My father threw in the towel, since he'd been offered a job by one of the big milk co-ops. We moved to Burlington. The Tylers, from what David tells me, didn't come to Dabney till ten or twelve years after we were long gone. I saw the girl at the studio last night. That's all."

"But you and Mr. Hale have been close all these years."

Walberg looked at David. He was David's faithful gofor, the adoring fat spaniel, Quist thought.

"David and I hardly knew each other at all in high school," Pudge said. "He played sports and was one of the most popular boys. I was a sort of misfit. But he was very decent to me at the time of the rumble over Mr. Short."

"Pudge blamed himself for what happened," David said.

"I told Mrs. Avery where she could find Mr. Short," Pudge said.

"That made no sense," David said. "Short and Teddy Williams would have been caught out sooner or later. Miss Moffet asked me to try to make Pudge see that he shouldn't blame himself. I did what I could. But after the Walbergs moved away I didn't see him for a good many years." David glanced at Peggy. "I'd been married, gone to Hollywood, been divorced, and come back to New York. A good fifteen years, I guess. Peg and I had just remarried when I ran across Pudge at the television studio where I was doing my news show. He was looking for a job and I gave him one. Boyhood friend. He's been with me ever since. What is it now, Pudge, almost five years?"

Walberg nodded.

The telephone rang and Lydia picked up the instrument that rested on the end of the little bar. Her face took on a strained look as she held it out to Quist.

"Walter Nichols for you, Julian," she said.

Quist felt a twinge of sadness as he took the phone from Lydia. He thought he knew what Nick would have to tell him. Esther Moffet hadn't made it.

But that wasn't it. Esther was still unconscious, still critical, still a long shot, but still alive.

"We've had another violence in Dabney, Julian. I thought you ought to know." Old Nick sounded exhausted and more than a little shaken. "It must have happened in the night, although I only got word a little while ago. People didn't know where I was."

"What is it, Nick?"

"Sam Hamner," the old man said. "You remember? The lawyer who defended Robert Short and was later David Halstrohm's guardian?"

"A 'vegetable,' you said."

"His house was torn apart, just like Esther's. His night nurse was struck down from behind—that famous 'blunt instrument' they always talk about. This guy doesn't just tap you, Julian, but she got one quick look at him before he slugged her. Like you thought, a stocking mask. Sam is dead."

"Beaten up?"

"No. Either he just died peacefully in his sleep, a coincidence, or he died from the effort of trying to yell for help. You know, Julian, I'm kind of getting a message."

"Oh?"

"Here in Dabney it isn't too safe to know anything about the Short case. How is it down your way?"

While Quist was giving the gist of Old Nick's message to Kreevich and the others, the gathering was augmented by the arrival of Dan Garvey and Connie Parmalee, Quist's secretary.

"I'm late because I was trying to produce that miracle for you," Garvey said. "No dice. I found a friend willing to take a casual look at local Social Security records. No woman named Short was paying in to Social Security in the city in the late forties. Of course, there are fifty other States, but I can't get to national records until tomorrow."

Quist hadn't really hoped for that kind of break.

"What the hell is going on?" Garvey wanted to know. "You think it was Laverick's man who beat up your Miss Moffet? This second one, too?"

Kreevich had gone to the phone to make a call while Garvey and Connie were being greeted. He came back into the gathering again.

"Joe Malik got back into town an hour and a half ago," he said. "He garaged Laverick's car and went straight to the great man's penthouse. That's where he is now." Kreevich made an impatient gesture. "I can have him tailed, but I don't have any grounds on which to pick him up. And I have my doubts about him, anyway."

"Doubts?" Quist's anger was hot. "He shows up in Dabney and two houses are torn apart and two women beaten up. He discards clothes somewhere because they must have been bloodstained. What room is there for doubts, Mark?"

David, who had been jolted by the news about his old friend Hamner, joined in. "We heard Laverick say he was going to 'turn the mice loose,' " he said. "What he meant was that if somebody had something on me he was going to make sure about it himself. But this kind of violence when there's nothing to find out! Have you an explanation for that, Julian?"

"Not yet," Quist said.

"Let me give you a line on Joe Malik," Kreevich said. "He's a man with a reputation, most of it violent. He was an agent for the CIA for some fifteen years. That's where the violence was, most of it abroad—Europe, South America. He got such a reputation for strong-arm methods that the CIA finally let him go. Laverick hired him. Laverick Enterprises is one of the most powerful multinational conglomorates. A man of Malik's experience and cold-blooded ferocity is just the kind of guy the Lavericks of this world need when they get to the infighting. Malik is a professional and not some kind of improvising amateur."

"Well, he's torn apart the village of Dabney and is now sitting calmly in Laverick's penthouse telling him about it. And neither you nor the Vermont state police can touch him. That's professional, isn't it?"

"There's one other thing that makes for doubts," Kreevich said. "A World War Two vintage German Luger. That's what killed Abbie Tyler. Unless we're looking for a whole army of strong-arm guys, then we'd have to guess the man who's been raising hell in Dabney is the man who killed

Abbie Tyler. And you can be pretty damn sure Joe Malik wouldn't use a World War Two German Luger on a job. He would have a very modern, very efficient handgun."

"What killed that poor kid was efficient enough," Garvey muttered.

"Unless," Kreevich said, turning to David, "you had a souvenir gun in your apartment, Hale, and he used it instead of his own. You didn't forget to mention that, did you?"

"I don't own a gun of any kind, Lieutenant," David said.

"Julian had a theory about all this while we were in Vermont," Lydia said. "Two people or two sets of people."

"So?" Kreevich said.

Quist walked over to the bar and poured himself a slug of straight whiskey. He turned back. "The letters and the snapshots keep coming," he said, "particularly to me. I'm being teased into looking for something about David, something about the Short case. I'm doing well, according to the sonofabitch who's sending them. Would the same person keep getting in my way? Somebody wants me to uncover something. Somebody else wants to stop it. I was on my way to ask Miss Moffet for employment records on Short. We found her beaten and her place ripped apart. A search for those records? Sam Hamner might have kept records on the case at his home. His place is wrecked. Two forces; two sets of people."

"And you're in the middle," Garvey said.

"There is nothing to find out about me," David said. He sounded anguished. "There is nothing to hide that would hurt me. I keep telling all of you this, over and over."

"I wouldn't have gone looking for something if I hadn't believed there might be," Quist said. "You're my friend. I wanted to help you in spite of the fact that you weren't telling me everything you know."

"I appreciate that, Julian, deeply. But there is nothing to

find. And there is no reason why anyone connected with me —Laverick, Betz and Smallwood, the network people, my staff, my friends, for God sake—would go to such lengths to stop you from finding something that isn't there to find."

"So somebody used your friendship for David to get you to pry into the Short case hoping you would find something else, something that would incriminate somebody else," Garvey said. "David was just the bait."

"And somebody will commit murder to stop you," Kreevich said, his eyes narrowed.

"The south of France," Lydia said. Only Quist knew what she meant.

"There is someone who turned you on about David," Connie Parmalee said, her eyes hidden behind the tinted glasses. "I said I'd do some checking on Max Robson for you, boss. It may mean nothing, but I found out that Robson is a skiing nut."

"What the hell has skiing got to do with all this?" Quist asked, impatiently.

"Probably nothing, except that this last spring his favorite weekend place was Skytop Lodge," Connie said. "And Skytop Lodge is in the township of Dabney, Vermont."

Bits and pieces of a puzzle, not enough to make a picture, but tantalizing.

"Anything on Janice Trail?" Quist asked.

Connie glanced at David. "The lady's life is an open book," she said. "She finished a film about ten days ago on the Coast. She's been working on it for more than a year. The Lockwood novel, a superspecial. She came East and is staying at the St. Regis. Robson's doing a magazine feature on her, part of the publicity on the film. She's been to all the right plays, all the right parties—including David's. Robson brought her to that and got a special press release on it that has the gossip swallowers happy. Nothing to tie her into

Dabney or Skytop."

"She couldn't have been ten years old when the Short case happened," Peggy Hale said. Her smile was bitter. "Oh, I know how old she is."

Quist turned to David. "Why does Robson hate you so much?" he asked. "He went out of his way to blast your opening with a piece he wrote before it had even happened. He made a scene about you in Willard's Back Yard when Dan and Lydia and I were lunching there yesterday. Why does he want to damage you, David?"

David reached out to his wife. "Once, a long time ago, before either Max or I had made it, we had a run-in," he said. "I was making TV commercials in Hollywood. He was trying to catch on as a free-lance scriptwriter. I didn't know him, but at a party he made a lousy pass at Peg."

"You might call it attempted rape," Peggy said. "David flattened him. Threw him out of the apartment where we were in front of all his friends. He kept screaming he'd get even."

"Maybe that's just what he's trying to do," Quist said. A kind of fierce anger was churning in him. He was being used by someone. He had allowed himself to be challenged by this poison-pen bastard. He had gone hunting for some kind of nonexistent dirt on David, led to Dabney by the nose. Someone had hoped that while he searched for something to hurt David that wasn't there, he would uncover something that would destroy someone else. That someone else had been so determined to prevent it that he had killed Abbie Tyler in cold blood, beaten Miss Moffet to the edge of her grave, and frightened Samuel Hamner to death. And there was no sign that the ball game was over. If they moved again in the direction of the long-gone Robert Short, they could expect new violence. He turned his pale angry eyes to Kreevich.

"You've had thirty-six hours on the Tyler case, Mark.

How close are you to an answer?"

"Nowhere, to be honest," Kreevich said. "We know the kind of gun that was used, but we haven't got it. We know how the killer came and went—through the back garden. But there isn't a fingerprint in that apartment that we can't account for and that doesn't belong to people with alibis. We don't know where the Tyler girl got that snapshot."

"You call the Vermont state police and I'll give you hundred-to-one odds there are no fingerprints in Miss Moffet's cottage or Hamner's," Quist said. "Professional. You're having Joe Malik tailed, Joe Malik, professional, but after he's done his job in Dabney, and you've got no legal grounds to pick him up. Unless the Vermont troopers can find those bloody clothes—and it could take them months—Malik is home free. It's just possible if I'd thrown away that first letter I got, none of this would have happened."

"You're not blaming yourself for what happened to the Tyler girl, are you?" Kreevich asked.

"I made friends with her, I danced with her, and she's dead. I made friends with Esther Moffet, and she may be dead while we're talking about her. I wanted to know what Sam Hamner knew about the Short case, and he's dead. I've got cold sweat on my back when I think of Walter Nichols. He may be next. And Dan and Connie, who've done a little snooping. Well, Mark, I don't have to be held back by any legal niceties. I'm going after this letter-writing monster who started it all in my own illegal way. And I'm going after Gerald Laverick himself, if that's where it leads."

"Laverick!" Kreevich sounded startled.

"Joe Malik works for him, doesn't he?" Quist said.

Part Three

ONE

Evening had descended on the city. From the terrace of Quist's apartment a mass of lights was spread out below, the lights from a thousand windows, the lights of homeward-bound weekend traffic on the East River Drive, the lights of slow-moving boats on the river itself. The bleak ugliness of the city, the garishness of its new architecture, was blotted out into a mass of shapes and shadows. The magic brightness of the stars faded in competition with a hundred million light bulbs.

Quist stood leaning on the iron guard rail, staring out at the city as though he thought he could force himself to see something that insisted on remaining hidden. Dan Garvey was stretched out in a deck chair, a drink resting on the flagstones beside him, studying Quist's tense figure.

"Sometimes in my association with you, Julian," he said, "I'm led to believe that you haven't got all your marbles."

Quist muttered something, as though he'd only half heard. Kreevich had gone, back onto the cold trail of Abbie Tyler's killer. He had left with warnings to Quist to attend to his own business and leave crime to the law. The Hales and Walberg had gone late to a meeting of David's staff to prepare for Monday night's show, which was to feature an Arab diplomat on the subjects of Middle East politics and oil. Lydia and Connie were in the kitchenette making sandwiches and coffee.

"You're a nice guy," Garvey said. "You got yourself involved in this because a friend was in trouble and because a nice little chick with a broken dress strap got herself killed. You did what a nice guy could do, but now, buster, you're in over your head."

Quist didn't move, but he spoke in a flat, cold voice. "Will you help me, Dan?"

"You know I'll help you, you sonofabitch!" Garvey made an impatient gesture. "I'll help you because I love you, and because Lydia loves you, and because Connie loves you—and God knows how many other people who need you and depend on you. That's why I'll help you. Not because you make one frigging bit of sense! Somebody should have washed out your mouth with soap when you mentioned Laverick's name. You're out of your league."

"What is my league?" Quist asked, not turning his head, staring out at the impersonal, blinking lights.

"You're the best damned public relations man in the history of the business," Garvey said. He sounded angry. "You could teach Laverick a hundred tricks for improving the images of the thousand companies he owns. You could make him look like a good guy if you wanted to, and that's nothing short of genius. You could make his phony Christer morality look like sainthood, if you wanted to. But when it comes to power and force and cold-blooded violence, Julian, you're a kindergarten kid playing with a mad dog!"

Quist turned his head, slowly. "You think as I do that Laverick is behind all this?"

"He was going to turn the mice loose to find the cheese, he said. We thought the cheese was something that would discredit David. It looks now as if the cheese was something that, if we looked into David's past, would damage someone else, not David. Laverick sends his man Malik to make sure that you don't stumble on the particular cheese that matters to him."

"The letter writer knows what that particular cheese is," Quist said.

"And he damn well better stay anonymous or Laverick will have him and his letters in the nearest shredding machine. You haven't got a real lead to anything, Julian, and if you get one Laverick will come down on you with all the force of his empire. You'll be dead before you can even run up a flag of distress."

"But you'll help?"

"Yes, you bastard, I'll help if you have the remotest idea how."

Quist turned around from the railing. He looked drawn and tired. "I'm particularly concerned about Walter Nichols and Lydia," he said. "They've both been openly involved with me in trying to dig out whatever there is to find in Dabney. Lydia we can watch out for, but we don't have bodyguards we can send to Dabney to protect the old man."

"You can't watch out for anybody if you don't know where the attack is coming from," Garvey said. "There's one thing that just doesn't make sense to me, Julian. If Laverick is behind this violence, why would he be so open about it? Why send Malik to Dabney, have him stay at the same hotel with you, let himself be seen by you, quite openly, in the hotel dining room. He might just as well have painted a road sign pointing to Laverick."

" 'Will you walk into my parlor?' said the spider to the fly.' Am I supposed to charge into Laverick's fortress and throw accusations around? In the course of which he would discover how much I know."

"Which at this moment is almost precisely nothing."

"You used the words 'mad dog,' " Quist said. "There was a mad dog loose in Dabney last night, and he's still at large."

"Then let the dog catcher get him," Garvey said. "You're not equipped."

It was a merry-go-round of an argument, Garvey knew. No one, not even Lydia, would talk Quist into backing away from what he thought was a just fight.

Lydia and Connie came out onto the terrace with trays of sandwiches and coffee, and an iced bottle of Chablis. The two women knew Quist well enough to be aware of what was cooking with him even though they hadn't overheard the discussion.

Connie sat down next to Garvey, her lovely long legs stretched out in front of her, her eyes behind the tinted lenses of her granny glasses narrowed against the smoke from her cigarette. She didn't seem interested in the food she'd helped prepare.

"You'll tell me I read too many suspense novels," she said to no one in particular.

"Maybe you do," Garvey said. "But fiction might be a little more entertaining than the few facts we've got."

"Woman's intuition and all that," Connie said.

"So rap on," Garvey said, impatient.

"You're pretty convinced that one hand in this game is being played by Laverick," Connie said.

"Julian is."

"But you haven't come up with any theories about the letter writer." She looked at Julian. "He has to be someone who knows the kind of guy you are, boss, the kind of bait you'd take."

"So?"

"He has to be someone who likes to play games with words."

"Item two," Garvey said.

"He has to be someone who was in Dabney at eleven o'clock yesterday morning or had a friend there. That's when one of the letters was mailed to you, boss."

"Item three, none of it news."

"All the letters to you, boss, and to the other people who got them the night of the party are typewritten. Most likely on the same typewriter, wouldn't you say?"

"A fair assumption," Quist said.

"So there is someone who knows all about you, boss, who could have had a friend in Dabney on Saturday morning, and whose business is words. We can't put him in jail because he meets all those requirements but there might be a way to prove he wrote the letters, and that would do him in, wouldn't it?"

Quist stood very straight and still. "You're talking about Max Robson, aren't you?"

"Not unnatural. I've been researching him all weekend," Connie said. A tiny smile moved her wide mouth. "He writes a syndicated column of criticism and comment each week."

"Loaded with mean little nasty words," Lydia said.

"It's not what he writes but where he writes it that interests me," Connie said. "Does he type his column at home or does he do it on a machine in the syndicate's offices? Either way it shouldn't be too difficult to get hold of an original copy of one of his manuscripts. There's a young man on the editorial staff there who's been trying to get me to look at his etchings for months. I think I could get hold of one of Robson's typescripts. If it turns out they're written on the same typewriter as the letters you've gotten, boss . . ."

"Your letter writer hates David," Lydia said.

"Or pretends to," Quist said.

"Robson hates David and that's not pretending," Garvey said.

"It's a long, very unlikely shot," Quist said. "Almost too easy."

"But I'll never forgive myself if I don't find out for sure," Connie said. "Unless you object?"

"Object! My dear, sweet girl!"

Connie stood up. "I'd better go home and get my beauty sleep if I'm going to be ready for etchings," she said. She paused by Quist, resisting the impulse to reach out and touch him. "I once read a book," she said, "about a big multinational conglomorate like Laverick Enterprises. The president of the company had a motto on his wall, a quote from John Maynard Keynes, the famous British economist. I remembered it because it seemed to say something about the world we're living in."

"You'll quote it whether we want to hear it or not," Garvey said.

"Lord Keynes said: 'For at least another hundred years we must pretend to ourselves and to everyone that fair is foul and foul is fair; for foul is useful and fair is not.' That's the way Laverick will fight you, boss. And when it's all over most people will believe that he was right and you were wrong. Is it worth it?"

"Amen," Lydia said.

Quist gave Lydia a tight little smile. "Just before I dive heroically off the top of the Empire State Building, let me try to make something clear to all of you. I know that dead heroes don't have much meaning. Whatever I do isn't meant to make me look good to you or anyone else. But nice, uncomplicated people are being bloodied and I was suckered into putting some of it into motion. In our society today eyewitnesses to crime lock themselves in the john and pretend they never saw what they saw. I just can't play it that way, kids. If what we have is Robson and Laverick sniping at each other, I'm going to do what I can to see that no one else gets caught in the crossfire."

"So I better find out fast if it is Robson," Connie said.

"I'll see you home, doll," Garvey said. "Being connected with this lunatic may make all of us targets."

*   *   *

Quist and Lydia were alone. Normally it was a very special time for them, the end of high-pressured days, a relaxed-in-love time. Tonight it was different. There were tensions neither one of them could ignore. They were simple and uncomplicated tensions for Lydia. She was afraid for Quist. For Quist it was more complex. He was afraid for a lot of people, frustrated by not having a clear course of action to follow.

The old newspaperman in Dabney was one of his top concerns, and as soon as Garvey and Connie had left he went to the phone and called Nichols' number in Vermont. There was no answer. He called Dabney's resident state trooper and got the woman he had talked to once before. She was, as he had suspected, Spofford's wife. The trooper was out on his regular evening patrol. It would take her a little time to reach him.

"I'm concerned about Walter Nichols," Quist told Mrs. Spofford. "He doesn't answer his phone."

"I think I heard my husband say he planned to go back to the hospital in Bennington."

"Of course, I should have thought of that," Quist said. "I'll check. But I'd appreciate it very much if your husband would call me, collect, when you can contact him. He has my number."

A call to the hospital in Bennington revealed two facts. Old Nick was not there, and Miss Esther Moffet was "doing as well as can be expected," which meant, at least, that she was still alive.

"Why are you so worried about Nick?" Lydia asked. She knew the answer but you couldn't live in silence.

"He feels the same way as I do about Abbie's killer," Quist said. "He wants to get him. He's digging. Someone may try to stop him from finding out who mailed that letter to me." He looked at this woman he loved, a deep frown splitting his forehead. "I don't want you involved in this, Lydia. It's bad enough that you went with me to Vermont, that Joe Malik saw you there. I'd like it if you could go somewhere for a few days, just stay out of sight, don't go to the office, don't come here. Your own apartment is listed in the phone book, so that's no good either."

"Why would they be interested in me?"

"Because you're mine," Quist said. "Because whatever I know they'll assume I've told you."

"But you don't know anything, not for certain!"

"One little extra piece that could nail Laverick could set a tornado in motion. You could hole up in a hotel for a couple of days. We could be in constant touch by phone. I'd like it if you would pack some things and I took you somewhere now, tonight."

"Julian, I don't want to leave you. If there's danger I want to share it with you. I don't want to be locked in a closet somewhere while you run the risks."

"I know." He reached out and touched her cheek. "But I can't move intelligently if I have to be concerned about your safety every second. Let me call Jerry Dodd. He's the security officer at the Hotel Beaumont. He'll arrange for a room for you and for you to register under some other name. Just for a day or two."

"Julian, I—"

The phone rang. It seemed soon for Spofford to be getting back to him, but Quist hurried to the instrument on the bar. It was the police, but not Spofford. Lieutenant Kreevich spoke in a cold, harsh voice.

"You been listening to your radio or watching TV?" he asked.

"No. Why?"

"We have a dead lady," Kreevich said.

Quist's heart sank. "Miss Moffet?"

"A retired New England schoolteacher doesn't rate network coverage," Kreevich said. "The dead lady is Janice Trail."

"*What!*"

"Somebody got into her room at the St. Regis, bashed in her skull, and made off with what her agent tells us may have been two hundred thousand dollars worth of jewelry. In spite of urgings Miss Trail wouldn't leave her pretties in the hotel safe."

"Nice city to live in," Quist said.

"You've got me thinking in circles," Kreevich said, "so let me tell you what I found myself playing with when I heard about Miss Trail. We have a dead man twenty-five years ago named Short, a friend of David Hale's; we have two men named Williams killed in a hunting accident nineteen years ago, friends of David Hale's; we have a retired schoolteacher beaten to a pulp, David Hale's high school principal; we have a sick old man frightened to death, David Hale's lawyer and guardian; and now we have Janice Trail, David Hale's one-time mistress. Coincidence, you think?"

"It's hard to think so. But people who are careless with jewelry have always been targets."

"You want to know where else my circular thinking took me?" Kreevich asked in that same, harsh voice. "If someone wants to wipe out everyone connected with David Hale, there are still David Hale's wife, David Hale's old school chum named Walberg, David Hale's public relations man and that man's organization. Quist is the name, isn't it? Then there's David Hale's old hometown friend, the editor of a newspaper, named Walter Nichols. Then there's a whole staff of people working on a TV show. And there's David Hale himself. God damn it, Julian, don't you see that all these people have got to lie low, stop trying to solve mysteries for themselves, and leave it to the stupid cops?"

"Do you know where Joe Malik was when Janice Trail

was robbed?" Quist asked.

"So you don't want to answer my question, so don't answer it, you stupid jerk," Kreevich said. "You want to play cops-and-robbers and risk your own life and the lives of people you care for, like that gorgeous broad of yours, it's your funeral—and maybe theirs. Yes, I know where Joe Malik was when Janice Trail was murdered. Robbery is supposed to be the motive for what happened, Julian. What happened was murder. Joe Malik hasn't left the fortress Laverick all night. The only thing we know for certain about the murder of our movie star is that the killer *wasn't* Joe Malik."

Quist didn't speak. Lydia had moved close to him and he put his free arm around her and held her close.

"So what are you going to do?" Kreevich wanted to know.

"I'm going to stash Lydia away someplace safe," Quist said.

"And then?"

"Mark, do you expect me to just sit here and wait for the boom to be lowered? It's too late for me to back off. I know too much already."

"I wish I knew what you know that could be any damned use to anyone. When all you've got are theories you're playing with dynamite, friend. Okay! You want flowers at the funeral or do you have a favorite charity?" The policeman banged down the receiver on the other end.

Without letting Lydia leave the comfort of his arm, Quist dialed the number of the Beaumont. It was fresh in his memory from making constant calls in the past week to make preparations for the party for David. He was put through promptly to Jerry Dodd, the hotel's security chief.

"A favor and help, Jerry," he said.

"Why not?"

"There isn't time for me to explain to you why, except that someone may be gunning for me and mine. I want to check Miss Morton into the hotel tonight, now, under a phony name. She may want to stay several days. I need your people to keep an eye on her."

"Say no more," Dodd said. "There'll be a house seat for —shall we say Miss Lee Smith?—when she gets here."

"House seat?"

"Hotel slang," Dodd said. "No matter how full up we are there's always a room or two open for special friends. We call 'em 'house seats,' like in the theater. You bringing the lady?"

"As far as the front door," Quist said. "I don't want her seen with me in the lobby—just in case. She'll go to the desk and ask for a reservation for Lee Smith."

"I'll be waiting," Dodd said. "What are you expecting, Mr. Quist?"

"Dan Garvey has described him as a mad-dog killer," Quist said.

"Get her here and she'll be safe," Dodd said. "Police in on this?"

"Yes and no," Quist said.

Dodd laughed. "You'll tell me what this is all about when you have time or I'll cut your heart out."

"Someone may beat you to it," Quist said.

He put down the phone and took Lydia's anxious face between his two hands. He moved his lips gently against hers.

"No arguments," he said after a moment. "We'll have a quick nightcap and then you'll pack some things and I'll take you to the Beaumont. Dodd can be trusted." He moved behind the bar and poured them each a drink on the rocks, a Scotch for Lydia and bourbon for himself.

"I didn't hear all that Kreevich said to you, Julian," Lydia said. "But why Janice Trail?"

"Mark suggests that someone has set out to eliminate everyone who has any close connection to David."

"That's pretty preposterous, isn't it?"

"Is there anything about this that isn't out of sight?"

Lydia sipped her drink, her violet eyes dark with concern. "Julian, you remember that you have a gun in your bureau drawer upstairs," she said.

She could have argued, pleaded with him, but she didn't and he loved her for it. They finished their drinks and he kissed her and she went upstairs to the room where she kept clothes and toilet articles. The bag was there she'd taken to Vermont with her.

Quist went up to his own room and collected the Police Special from his handkerchief drawer. He had a license for it. He checked the loading and slipped it into the pocket of his summer-weight tweed jacket. He glanced at himself in the mirror over the bureau and was shocked to see that his eyes looked sunk into dark holes in his face. He realized he'd had almost no sleep for two nights. He felt as tired as he looked.

In the mirror he saw the reflection of the little red light blinking on the bedside phone. He went over and picked it up. It was the collect call from Spofford in Dabney.

"My wife tells me you are worried about Old Nick," the trooper said. "You probably found out he isn't at the hospital."

"Yes, I did."

"Well, I haven't been able to locate him," Spofford said. "I was surprised he hadn't left a number at the hospital where he could be reached—in case anything went wrong with Miss Esther."

"Has anything?"

"No. She's a game old girl. The doctors are surprised she's made it this far. The longer she hangs on the better the chances. But about Mr. Nichols—what's worrying you?"

"There's been more violence here in town," Quist said. "This time we know it wasn't Joe Malik, but the man we think may be at the back of it has an army at his disposal. We think it ties into Dabney and the old Short case and to anyone who might be interested in it. Mr. Nichols is."

"Well, it's only just eleven o'clock," Spofford said. "He could be visiting with any one of a dozen friends in town. As soon as I catch up with him I'll warn him."

"Warning isn't enough," Quist said. "He needs protecting. If you haven't got the authority, Spofford, or you think I'm some kind of a crackpot, I'll have the police here call your superiors."

"Might be a good idea," Spofford said. "But I'll take care of him tonight."

Lydia was standing in the doorway, bag in hand.

"That was Spofford?"

"Yes. No sign of Nick yet. He'll keep looking."

"Julian?"

"Yes, luv."

"This has to be? I mean, I feel safer here than anywhere else in the world."

"If I were going to be here I'd agree. One foxhole is as good as another. But I've got to have this out from top to bottom with David. There must be something he knows or has forgotten he knows. And he, too, has to be warned, Lydia. Laverick seems bent on wiping out David's world before we can put two and two together and come up with even a small part of the answer."

Lydia drew a deep breath. "So, I'm ready," she said.

They went down in the elevator together. He suggested that Lydia wait in the lobby while he tried to flag a cab. It was a beautiful, warm night. Sunday night traffic was light. From the river came the moaning sound of a boat whistle. Quist stood at the curb, looking for the roof light of an unoccupied cab. He was only vaguely aware of a car pulling out of a parking space down the block. As it came toward him he glanced idly at it, wondering if it was gypsy cab. It turned in toward the empty space in front of the building and it was then that Quist noticed that in addition to the driver there was a passenger in the back seat. The passenger was half leaning out of the open rear window and a street light glittered against the barrel of a machine pistol.

This was it, Quist thought.

It was a moment for instinct, not planning. Commando training in the Far East had taught him to make the rolling dive for safety. He hit the pavement hard and went over and over behind a parked car. He heard the gun being fired and the spatter of bullets against the stone front of the building and the shattering of glass in the car behind which he'd made his dive for safety. He felt a stinging sensation at his left cheek and guessed it was a ricochet that had hit him.

As he rolled over he saw Lydia and the uniformed doorman coming out of the building. He shouted at them to go back. He managed to get his handgun out of his pocket and got to a crouching position behind the car. The taillight of the would-be assassin's car was disappearing down the block.

It had all been so quick. He reached up and touched his cheek. His fingers came away bloodied. Then Lydia and the doorman were with him, the man dithering about calling the police, Lydia just whispering his name over and over.

"You're hit, darling," she said, finally.

"Just grazed. It's nothing." He fished a handkerchief out of his pocket and blotted at the wound with it. He turned to the man. "Dominic, I want a taxi. The police later. We have to get out of here."

The doorman blew a shrill blast on his whistle and up the street the yellow roof light of a taxi came toward them. No one else seemed to have heard the gunfire, or if they had they weren't planning to become involved.

"Did you get the license number, Mr. Quist?" the doorman asked.

"You have to be kidding, Dominic. I was ducking for my life. Report this to the cops. They can talk to me later."

Quist and Lydia got into the cab and headed toward the Beaumont. For a moment they sat close together, holding onto each other.

"It's for real," Lydia said, in a shaken voice. "In spite of everything I thought it couldn't be real for us. Things don't happen to us. Only to other people."

"Nothing has happened to us," Quist said, "except to have the hell scared out of us." He held her tight, and then he leaned away from her. He looked at his handkerchief and there was very little blood on it. An inch or two to the left and he'd have been minus an eye. "I'm not coming into the hotel with you, luv. And once you get there you're to stay in your room until I've talked to you. You want food or drink, ask Jerry Dodd for it. Have him or one of his people bring it to you. No room service people, no strangers."

"You'll call soon?"

"As soon as there's anything to call about."

"Julian, if you go openly to see David—"

"I only need to be warned once," Quist said grimly. The cab pulled up in front of the Beaumont. "Take it easy. I love you—Lee Smith."

"Your friend could have been more imaginative about a name," she said. "Smith!"

She kissed him and was gone, swallowed up in the Beaumont's lobby.

TWO

Quist gave the cab driver an address in the Murray Hill district. He needed help and advice and the use of a telephone that wasn't out in the open somewhere. The logical place to go for all three things was to his closest friend. Dan Garvey would scold, but he would make sense and he would help.

Quist paid off the cab outside the remodeled brownstone where Garvey lived. He rang the doorbell, but nothing happened. He stood with his finger on the bell for quite a while. Then Garvey's angry voice came through the speaker system.

"What the hell is it? Fire?"

"It's Julian. I need help, chum."

"Oh, Christ!" Then the release catch clicked and Quist let himself in and climbed the stairs to the second floor. Garvey was waiting at his door, wearing a terry-cloth robe, his feet bare. He was clearly irritated.

"Couldn't you call before you came?" he asked. He kept the doorway blocked.

"You're not alone?"

"That's my privilege, God damnit," Garvey said.

At any other time Quist would have been amused, but at any other time he would have called and he wouldn't have stood for five minutes with his finger on the doorbell.

"What the hell did you do to your face?" Garvey asked.

"Bullet from a machine pistol," Quist said.

Garvey's face hardened. He opened the door wide and Quist went in.

"Look, chum," Quist said, "let me go into the kitchen and make myself a drink and use the phone there. Apologize to the lady for me—and get rid of her. You know I wouldn't ask if it wasn't serious."

"Go," Garvey said.

Quist went into the kitchen and closed the door behind him. He knew where Garvey kept his liquor and he poured himself a stiff hooker that went down like water. He wondered if Garvey had brought Connie back here, or if the lady in the bedroom was a prior date. He poured a second drink and carried it to the phone. He tried to reach Kreevich. Headquarters reported the lieutenant was out on a case. They'd try to reach him. Quist gave them Garvey's number. Then he dialed David Hale's number. There was no response to the long ringing. He hadn't thought to ask David where the conference on tomorrow's show was being held. Then he recalled that David had an answering service. He called and gave his name.

"Oh, yes, Mr. Quist," the operator said. He had left messages before. "I don't know where David is. He hasn't called in this evening. But he usually does when he gets home, no matter how late."

"When he does, tell him it's urgent," Quist said. "I'm not at home but he may be able to reach me at this number." He gave the girl Garvey's number.

"Will do, Mr. Quist."

Then Quist called the Beaumont and asked for Miss Lee Smith. "It's me, luv," he said when Lydia answered.

"You're all right?"

"I'm fine. I'm at Dan's. Just wanted to make sure you were in and safe."

"This must be the suite for royalty," Lydia said. Her laugh was a little unnatural. "All I need is a bottle of champagne, a black negligee, and a man."

"Just hold that thought," Quist said.

The kitchen door opened and Garvey came in, wearing a pair of dark slacks, a navy blue turtleneck knit shirt, and loafers on his bare feet.

"So let's have it," Garvey said. "The lady may forgive you sometime in the distant future, by the way."

"You obviously haven't been watching television," Quist said. He told his friend what had happened to Janice Trail and what Kreevich had called his "circular thinking." People all connected with David Hale for the last twenty-five years. "And to back it up, somebody tried to gun me down outside my building. Thank God I'd left Lydia in the lobby while I tried to flag a cab. We couldn't both have escaped it."

"Bastards!" Garvey said. "You've told Kreevich?"

"Can't reach him. I've given him this number. I tried to call David to warn him, but he's out of touch."

"Lydia?"

"She's stashed away in the Beaumont, under the name of Lee Smith if you should have to call her."

"To tell her you died whispering her name? You damned idiot! Back off, Julian. Get out!"

"It's too late, Dan. The only way out would be to call Laverick and tell him I don't know anything. A man who's gone this far probably wouldn't risk believing me. The only way out is to nail him."

"How?"

"The letter writer knows what it is Laverick's trying to cover," Quist said. "If Connie's guess is correct, and it should happen to be Max Robson . . ."

"And if it isn't?"

"Then we keep trying to find out who it is. There's still the chance we can find out who mailed that letter to me in Dabney Saturday morning."

"I don't suppose you know whether you were followed here or not."

"Not," Quist said. "I had to be sure Lydia and I weren't tailed to the Beaumont. They may think they got me back at my building. I went down pretty quickly when they started shooting."

"So we wait for Connie to look at her friend's etchings."

"She's got to move faster than that. If I know Connie, she won't dawdle."

The phone rang and Garvey answered it. "Kreevich for you," he said, and handed Quist the phone.

Kreevich sounded like a snarling, angry stranger. "Where the hell are you? What is this number?"

"Dan Garvey's apartment."

"Address?"

Quist gave it to him.

"There'll be a police car there for you in five minutes. Your girl with you?"

"No. I think I ought to tell you, Mark. Somebody tried to gun me down outside my building. Lydia's in a safe place."

Kreevich's voice cracked. "This sonofabitch is trying to wipe out the whole town in one night. We've got another one, Julian."

"Who?"

"George Walberg, Hale's handyman."

"Where?"

"At the Hales' apartment. Shot in the head, place torn apart."

Quist felt a cold finger run down his spine. "The Hales?" he asked.

"They're not here," Kreevich said. "I hoped you could tell me where they might be. Weren't they supposed to be at some kind of conference on his show?"

"Micky Grant, the network man, would know."

"You hang up," Kreevich said. "I'll have the nearest patrol car pick you up. From now on you're going to play this my way. And you'd better bring Garvey. Who knows, he may be on the enemy list, too."

The Hales' apartment reminded Quist of what he'd seen in Esther Moffet's cottage in Dabney long hours ago. It had been ripped apart inch by inch, furniture, books, papers on the desk, china, cooking utensils.

Kreevich's special crew was there with cameras, fingerprint equipment, and miniature vacuum cleaners. An ambulance crew was just taking away Pudge Walberg's body when Quist and Garvey arrived in the patrol car Kreevich had sent for them. The outline of Pudge's body was chalked out on the living room rug. He had fallen just inside the front door.

"Looks like he'd answered the doorbell or a knock," Kreevich said. "Opened the door and was shot between the eyes before he could back off. What happened to your face?"

"That's how close I came to getting it just where Pudge got it," Quist said.

"What we have on our hands is a massacre," Kreevich said. He was white, tense, seething with anger. "Lucky you, but don't count on your luck holding."

"Could Micky Grant tell you where the conference is being held?"

"Broke up an hour ago," Kreevich said. "Grant supposed the Hales would be here at home. If they had been here, we'd have to guess they'd be dead."

"So you have to find them so they don't walk into an ambush."

"I don't need instructions on how to do my job," Kreevich said. Then he shook his head slowly from side to side. "Sorry,

Julian, but this one has got me off my rocker. Tell me about Walberg."

"You heard his story. As for his job, it was to make life easier for David—run errands, keep people out of his hair when he was working. It calls for a special kind of devotion."

"It doesn't help to know anything except that he was connected to David Hale, like everyone else so far," Kreevich said.

"So far?"

"Is it likely to stop? They missed you, but they'll be back, won't they? What the hell are they looking for—here and in those two houses in Dabney?"

"Something Laverick has to hide," Quist said.

Kreevich made an impatient gesture. "You still buy your Laverick theory? You haven't got anything on him, you know. His man was in Dabney, quite openly. Ate breakfast in the same dining room with you. Knew you'd recognize him. Laverick announced he was going to check on David's past."

"There are the bloody clothes," Quist said.

"God damn it, you haven't got any bloody clothes. I played along with this theory, Julian, and the result is close to proving it doesn't make sense. Joe Malik didn't kill Janice Trail and he didn't do this. I know exactly where he is. He's in Laverick's penthouse on top of the Laverick Building on Park Avenue. He hasn't left there since he got back from Vermont in the early afternoon. What the hell connection could Gerald Laverick have with a queer who got arrested for molesting a kid twenty-five years ago?"

"If we had the answer to that, Mark, you could walk in and arrest him," Quist said. "You ask what they were searching for here and at the two places in Vermont. Maybe it's something that would show Laverick's connection with Robert Short."

"Nobody searched this place when the Tyler girl was shot," Kreevich said.

"She scared them off by forcing them to fire at her. That Luger must have sounded like a cannon going off in here," Quist said. "Was Walberg shot with a Luger?"

"Have to wait for ballistics, but from the look of the wound, I'd say not."

Quist brought a fist down into the palm of his other hand. "We've got to locate David and Peggy," he said.

The phone on the foyer table rang and Kreevich answered it. It turned out to be Micky Grant, anxious to know whether the Hales had turned up safe and sound.

"I got thinking," Grant said, when he'd been told they hadn't. "They left the conference with Pudge. Pudge drove their car for them. The last thing they said was that after the kind of day it had been they had to get home and get some sleep. Didn't the doorman say whether they were with Pudge?"

"Doorman?"

"Sure. There's a night man there in the lobby, all night."

Kreevich began to indulge in a slow, methodical stream of profanity. Of course, there had been a night man there when the Hales had found Abbie Tyler. Kreevich had talked to the man himself. He hadn't heard the shot that had killed Abbie, because he'd been helping some drunk in out of a taxi. There'd been no sign of any night man here tonight. Kreevich sent a couple of his men to search the basement and the service areas.

"Who let you know about Walberg?" Quist asked him.

"Nobody let me know. I found him myself. After the Trail thing broke at the St. Regis I figured the Hales were in trouble. They didn't answer their phone so I came over. The apartment door was standing open so I walked in. Damn near fell over Walberg."

There was a night man. He was a half-dead night man. Kreevich's cops found him in the basement. He had been severely beaten and locked up in a broom closet. After some first aid treatment he had a short story to tell. The Hales and Walberg had come in shortly after eleven o'clock, said goodnight, gone into the apartment. Walberg often stayed with them, the man said. About ten minutes later three or four men came into the lobby—maybe five or six.

"Like a frigging army," the man said through broken teeth and swollen lips. "They all had on like stocking masks or ski masks. No faces."

Esther Moffet's attacker had worn a stocking mask, Quist remembered. A uniform for executioners.

The night man had been slugged, dragged down the stairs to the basement. He'd heard a gun shot, and then the world had caved in on him.

Pudge must have opened the door to the stocking-faced army. He would have tried to stop them. He would have—had, in fact—given his life for David.

"You have to think the Hales were here and were taken away," Quist said.

"Why?" Garvey asked, speaking for the first time.

"They didn't find what they were looking for." Kreevich answered the question. "They took the Hales somewhere they'd have time to force them to talk."

"So you can add two more corpses to your collection," Garvey said. "Mad-dog Sunday!"

Quist was looking down at the chalk outline of Pudge Walberg's body on the rug. The whole chain of violence was unbelievable. Mad dog was the right word for it. Or was it? A mad dog runs wild, attacking anyone in his path, but here there was a kind of design, a kind of connection between each crime. The victims were all friends of David's, and except for Janice Trail, so far as Quist knew, they had all been involved in some fashion with the tragedy of Robert Short twenty-five years ago. Not himself, of course, but he'd been digging into the old case which linked him to it. Mad, perhaps, but not mad dog. There was a pattern, a violent purpose behind all this. Unless they could get a glimmer of what it was, it would go on until everyone who was touched by or who touched the Short case would be rubbed out.

Garvey helped to make up Quist's mind. Like Quist and Kreevich he was anchored near the front door of the wrecked apartment, wanting to back away from it. Wanting, he admitted to Quist later, to run away from it—run just as far as he could to some place that was safe.

"I have to buy Julian's theory about Laverick," he said. "Malik's alibi for tonight is just his alibi. There were two men in the car that tried to gun down Julian. There were maybe half a dozen men here. Our beat-up night man said it; an army. Who has armies in this day and age? The Syndicate, the Mafia, whatever you want to call them? This doesn't smell like organized crime, Kreevich. It's too reckless, too widespread, too suddenly urgent. So what other kinds of people have an army?"

"The Lavericks of this world," Quist said.

"You've lost me," Kreevich said, not really lost but listening.

"The big multinational companies, the conglomerates," Garvey said. "The men who control the national resources, the economy, the governments of half the world. They buy and wheel and deal their way to power, and when that doesn't work they have their armies, their spies, their undercover operators, their assassins. What was that quote of Connie's from Lord Keynes? '. . . fair is foul and foul is fair; for foul is useful and fair is not.' So foul is useful to someone who has the manpower to carry it out. Laverick has something in common with everyone else in this stinking case. He has an involvement with David Hale and, through his man, he has been poking around in the village of Dabney, Vermont, the scene of the Short case.

"The letter writer sent him a letter and a snapshot," Quist said. "I suggest he recognized the snapshot and he set out to destroy any evidence about the Short case and any people who might have dangerous memories about it, and anyone who might be nosing around close to the truth."

"So why did the letter writer send him a letter," Kreevich asked, "if it would turn him so tough?"

"Blackmail," Garvey said.

"I think I'd like to walk up to his front door and face him," Quist said. "That ought to be a lot safer than letting him choose the time and place when we meet again."

"You can't get in to see him," Garvey said. "I know how his kind work, Julian. There's that fancy secretary of his, and then his lawyer, and two weeks from now you get word that he'll see you after Labor Day! You can't force your way in. His penthouse is on top of the forty-story Laverick Building. You couldn't get through the street door without being stopped."

"There is a way," Quist said.

"How?"

"Kreevich takes me in, police shield in hand. Now wait a minute, Mark, before you start screaming! You have a bloody Sunday on your hands. You connect it to the village of Dabney. Laverick's man Joe Malik was there, presumably to check on David's morals. What did he learn? Who did he talk to?"

"And did he beat up Miss Esther Moffet, knock Samuel Hamner's night nurse over the head and frighten Hamner to death, and wreck two houses?" Garvey asked.

"We don't suggest that," Quist said. "We tell him everything that's happened, everything we know, and listen to what he has to say. After that we play it by ear."

"We go to him for help," Kreevich said. A tight smile moved his lips.

"Right on."

"I'll buy it," Kreevich said. "If he's our man, we may get him to rethink a little about what comes next. If he isn't, then perhaps he can help us."

"Gerald Laverick helps nobody but himself," Quist said.

The Laverick Building is one of those modern glass-and-steel mammoths, thrusting itself skyward as if to defy some invisible power. Except for the street-level floor it was dark at this time of night, as if people and machines were turned off. It you had craned your neck to look up forty stories, you would not have seen that there were lights again in the elaborate penthouse. Laverick's living quarters were shielded by high walls that made it invisible except to the airborne.

The ground-floor level was all glass, except for the black steel beams that rose upward. It was brilliantly lighted so that there wasn't even a shadow in the vast lobby with its banks of elevators, its black directory boards with gold letters glittering. The lobby area was patrolled by uniformed guards, their holstered guns plainly visible. The Laverick empire had to be protected. In this building was Laverick's bank, the secret files and offices of a hundred great companies, records that could have changed the course of history if they were revealed to the wrong persons at the wrong time —the wrong persons and the wrong time from Gerald Laverick's point of view.

The Fortress Laverick, it had been called.

"There is even a helicopter pad on the roof," Kreevich said.

"So how good is Malik's alibi?" Quist asked.

Kreevich squinted up into the sky and they saw a chopper

circling the area. "No one's used the pad since Malik checked in," Kreevich said. "That's a police bird."

There were four of them now standing at the front entrance—Kreevich, Quist, Garvey, and a uniformed cop. They rang an almost concealed bell. Instantly two guards, the tan uniforms smartly tailored, came to the inside of the door. They made no move to open up. One of them took down a gold telephone instrument from the wall and a voice sounded just over Quist's head.

"There's a grill just over the bell you rang," the voice said. "Speak into it. What do you want?"

"To see Mr. Laverick," Kreevich said.

"You have to be kidding," the voice said.

The lieutenant took out the leather folder containing his police shield. "Lieutenant Kreevich, police department," he said.

"Who are the others?"

"Patrolman Kline, Mr. Quist and Mr. Garvey. Laverick knows them both."

"Wait," the voice said. The guard put down the gold telephone and walked away across the lobby. The other guard remained just inside the door, hand resting on the butt of his gun. It was a long wait, a very long wait. Finally, the first guard came back toward the door. He spoke into the gold phone.

"Mr. Laverick has retired for the night," he said. "But Mr. Crown, his counsel, will talk to you."

The first thing was to get in.

"We'll talk to Crown," Kreevich said.

The huge glass door opened, apparently untouched by human hands, and they went in.

"You'll have to turn over your guns," the guard said.

Kreevich's smile looked hopeful. "You take one step toward me or Patrolman Kline and we'll find out just how fast you are on the draw, buster."

"It's a routine precaution," the guard said. "But since you're the police—" He shrugged. "This way."

Their footsteps on the marble floor echoed hollowly as the guard led the way to the bank of elevators. He paused in front of one marked PRIVATE. The door slid open noiselessly. There was no one inside to have opened it.

Kreevich went in. Garvey happened to be next. Then Quist stepped forward and instantly there was the raucous sound of some kind of alarm bell.

"Hold it!" the guard shouted. "This man's carrying a gun."

Kreevich looked at Quist. "Are you?"

"Yes. And I have a license for it as you very well know."

"Let him have it," Kreevich said.

Quist turned his gun over to the guard and stepped into the elevator. Patrolman Kline, a burly pleasant-faced young man, followed him. The elevator door closed and the car started up. There was no control panel in the car, no buttons to stop you at a floor or reverse your direction. The car went up and up with an almost imperceptible swish of sound.

At last the car stopped and the door slid open. Four uniformed guards faced them, and standing behind them was Jason Crown, Laverick's legal aid.

Kreevich led the way out of the elevator and the door closed behind them.

"Mr. Quist, Mr. Garvey," Crown said, very polite. "And you are Lieutenant Kreevich?"

Kreevich showed his shield.

"This way, please," Crown said.

They were in a square, windowless marble-walled room. Up here there was only one elevator door. There were two plain benches on either side of another door that evidently led into the penthouse. This marble box was air conditioned.

Quist could see vents up toward the ceiling.

They were taken through the door between the benches and into an austere sort of reception room, furnished with a long stretcher table and a half dozen green leather chairs. Nothing else; not a picture, not a hanging, not a window. Air conditioning again. The guards had remained outside.

Crown faced them, his back to a far door. He didn't suggest that they sit down.

"You realize that it's after midnight, Lieutenant?" Crown asked. There were bright spots of color in his cheeks. He looked as if he'd been drinking more than a little. He was wearing gray slacks, a navy blue blazer, a white ascot scarf at his neck. He looked like a man who lived here.

"I've been able to tell time since my kindergarten days, Mr. Crown," Kreevich said. "Now, if you'll take us to Laverick."

"My dear fellow, Mr. Laverick is in bed. Nothing in God's world would persuade me to wake him." Crown tried a smile. "It would be worth my job."

"I'm going to ask you to risk it," Kreevich said.

"This is really quite extraordinary, Lieutenant."

"It's been an extraordinary day and night," Kreevich said. "And while you're waking Laverick, you might send Joe Malik in here for a little talk."

Crown fretted at his mouth with a shaky hand. "Well, I hardly think—"

"You might as well bring them in, Jason," a harsh, metallic-sounding voice said.

Quist looked up and saw the speaker in the corner of the room. They were wired for sound. The voice was Laverick's.

Crown gave the visitors a sickly smile. He was hired to make decisions and then not allowed to make them. The door behind him opened and they went into another bare, windowless room. Quist found himself vaguely reminded of the Pentagon and the Rayburn Building in Washington, mechanized, computerized, without beauty or grace or charm or humanity. This second room was like a dining hall for monks in a monastery; a long stretcher table with plain wooden chairs set around it. There were, however, no saints or virgins or figures on a cross to be seen. Only the appearance of the old man seated at the head of the table provided an eccentric touch. Gerald Laverick, with his shaved skull and his pale blue eyes bright with hate, wrapped in a gray flannel bathrobe, with felt slippers on his feet, was sipping a glass of milk as he watched them file in. Standing directly behind his chair, like a figure carved from rock, was Joe Malik.

"Good evening, gentlemen," Laverick said, and waved to the chairs around the table. Nobody accepted the invitation. "You needn't be concerned about having waked me. It is an excuse we use to unwelcome guests. As a matter of fact, I rarely sleep more than forty minutes at a time." The pale eyes fastened on Kreevich. "What has been so extraordinary about this day and night, Lieutenant?"

"As you know, in the early hours of Saturday morning a girl named Abbie Tyler was murdered in the Hales' apartment," Kreevich said, sounding almost matter-of-fact. "Saturday night or early this morning a woman named Esther Moffet was nearly beaten to death in her home in Dabney, Vermont, her house ransacked. That same night a sick man was frightened to death, his nurse beaten, his house turned upside down. Earlier this evening Janice Trail, the movie star, was murdered in her room at the St. Regis Hotel. Gunmen attempted to kill Mr. Quist a little later. After that the Hales' apartment was broken into by a group of masked men, George Walberg shot between the eyes, the apartment ripped to pieces, and the Hales spirited away. I don't know how much of this is news to you, Mr. Laverick, but you'll have to admit it constitutes a rather extraordinary day and night."

"And what has all this to do with me, Lieutenant?"

"You must be concerned," Kreevich said. "David Hale is a big investment for you, isn't he? All of the people I've mentioned were, like yourself, somehow involved with David Hale."

"Have you come to tell me I might be next on the list?" the old man asked. "If you have, you must have observed that I'm well protected here."

"Your man Malik was in Dabney at the time the two crimes were committed there," Kreevich said.

"So was Mr. Quist," Laverick said, with a smile that was more like a grimace.

"Why was Malik in Dabney?" Kreevich asked.

"That's no secret, Lieutenant. As Mr. Quist and Mr. Garvey have no doubt told you, I, along with some others, received a threatening letter along with an old snapshot. The letter suggested that there was something in David Hale's past that would make him an unprofitable investment for me. The picture was taken twenty-five years ago when Hale, or Halstrohm, his real name, was living in Dabney. I sent Malik to investigate."

"What did he find out?"

"He was able to identify the people in the picture, a man and a boy," Laverick said. "They were involved in an unpleasantness in the high school there twenty-five years ago. What was important to me was the information that David Hale was innocent of any immoral actions."

A muscle rippled along the line of Quist's jaw. "Who identified the snapshot for you, Malik?" he asked.

The bodyguard stood motionless, silent.

"Tell him, Joseph," Laverick said.

Malik shrugged. "I just showed it around in town," he

said. "Finally some guy recognized the people."

"What guy?"

"Fellow in the drugstore. I don't know who he was."

"Once Joseph knew who the people in the picture were, there was no difficulty running down the story," Laverick said.

"I find that interesting," Quist said, "because I had great difficulty running it down in detail."

"Joseph is a professional at this sort of thing."

"Fine. Then, of course, he knows where Robert Short's wife and son are."

"Joseph?"

"Nobody seemed to know," Malik said.

"Did you talk to Walter Nichols, who runs the newspaper there and is a sort of town historian?" Quist asked.

"No."

"Or to Miss Esther Moffet, who was principal of the school when the Short scandal broke?"

"No."

"Or to Samuel Hamner, who was Short's lawyer?"

"No."

"Of course, Miss Moffet and Hamner were attacked while you were there. Being a professional, isn't it strange that you didn't go to these primary sources, Malik? You just talked to some guy in the drugstore?"

"And others. People are eager to gossip in a small town like that," Malik said.

Laverick indulged in his abortive smile again. "Were you by any chance responsible, Mr. Quist, for having Joseph stopped on his way home by the police?"

"I was," Quist said. "I hoped they would find the clothes he wore when he attacked Miss Moffet. They would have had to be bloodstained."

"So that was it," Laverick said. "And are you here to

suggest that it was Joseph who killed the Trail woman, who shot at you, who murdered Walberg, and abducted the Hales?" He made a sound that was meant to be laughter.

"I know he wasn't responsible for what happened here in the city tonight," Kreevich said. "I know he hasn't left this building since he got back from Vermont in the early afternoon."

"Do you really think there's no way out of this place that you couldn't keep under surveillance, Lieutenant? Give me ten minutes' start and you can search this building from roof to subbasement and you won't find me. By the way, are those police helicopters that have been circling overhead for the last ten or twelve hours?"

"They are."

"You don't think of that as an invasion of privacy, Lieutenant?"

It was a stone wall. A few days of circulating in Dabney might reveal that Malik had talked to no one. In a few days someone might come up with the bloody clothes. But in a few days more people would almost certainly die, and David and Peggy Hale would be at the top of the list.

Quist changed his tack. "Does the name Robert Short mean anything to you, Mr. Laverick?"

"A fairy teacher who molested a little boy twenty-five years ago? Why on earth should it?"

"In your long career literally hundreds of thousands of people must have worked for you. Would your computerized records show whether Robert Short was ever one of them?"

"They would show," Laverick said, unconcerned.

"Would you check?"

"Jason!" Laverick said.

"First thing in the morning," Crown said.

"Tonight, Jason. In the next ten minutes."

Crown left the room.

Quist shifted his approach again. "Kidnaping has become a kind of national sport," he said. "For political reasons, or business reasons, or for revolutionary causes. It's just possible that's what's happened to the Hales. If there is a ransom demand, it may come to you. How far will you go to help David and his wife?"

The old man seemed to freeze. "Why should a demand come to me?" he asked.

"Because you have wealth and power in so many areas," Quist said.

Laverick hesitated a moment. Then he said: "Money I would consider. But nothing on earth could make me change a political stance or a business program."

"Not even to save lives?"

"Are you suggesting that David Hale is indispensable, or that anyone is indispensable, Mr. Quist? Not in my world."

"I guess it would be out of character for you to say anything else," Quist said.

Laverick turned to Kreevich, as if he were bored by Quist. "Is there anything sensible I can do for you, Lieutenant? I'm shocked by your bloody story, but I don't know how I can help you."

"Have you received a second letter from the man who sent the snapshot?"

"Of course not," Laverick said.

"What happens tonight?" Quist asked. "It is tonight now—Monday night. I'm talking about Night Talk, David's show."

"If he's missing, that's that," Laverick said.

"I think I'd like to go on the air in his place if David's still missing," Quist said. "I think I'd like to make a direct appeal to the kidnapers, who are bound to be listening to see what happens."

"I don't think I like it," Laverick said.

"Why not? You might just have the biggest audience that ever listened to a talk show. Your only concern is to have an audience for your advertising, isn't it?"

"You imagine yourself to be so popular?" Laverick asked.

"By tonight the whole country will know that there's been a mass killing. Johnny Carson could take the night off."

Crown came back into the room. "No Robert Short in the records, Mr. Laverick."

In a matter of minutes the computer had sifted through perhaps half a million names and come up empty—if that's how it had come up.

The uniformed guards were in the outer hall. The elevator door opened. They were swept down the long shaft to the main floor. In the brightly lighted lobby the guard there returned Quist's gun to him. They went out onto Park Avenue.

They were nowhere.

THREE

You can go only so far, endure only so much pressure without sleep. The four men stood out on the avenue and looked at each other.

"Nothing to go on," Kreevich said in a flat, harsh voice.

"He smells like rotting garbage!" Garvey said. "But how do you get at him? While there's a chance for David and his wife, you can't just blunder in."

"You can't blunder in, period!" Kreevich said. "You want to try to get back in there now? It would take a delegation from the governor and maybe an army tank. And by the time you were in, like he said, he would be gone."

"So Malik's alibi for the last hours is no good," Garvey said.

"It doesn't matter much. Two men tried to gun down Julian. Five or six broke into the Hale apartment. Malik is one foot soldier in an army."

"I want to check on Walter Nichols," Quist said. He scarcely recognized his own voice, it was so heavy with fatigue. "We've got to get him under cover. Dan, would you think of staying with me at my place?"

"Where they may be waiting for you? They know now they missed you."

"I've got to be where I can be reached," Quist said. "Nichols may try to call me. There might be something from Lydia. Connie may find out something. I've got to be where people can find me."

"You know I'll go with you," Garvey said.

Kreevich agreed only on the condition that cops would take them back to Beekman Place and search the place and that Quist wouldn't leave without checking.

"If someone gets killed I know is in danger, I'll be selling newspapers in Times Square next week," he said.

A patrol car with a team of cops took Quist and Garvey to Beekman Place. They went up to the duplex and searched both floors. While they were searching, Quist called Walter Nichols in Dabney without results. Then Spofford, who sounded sleepy.

"I tried to get you a half a dozen times, Mr. Quist."

"With news?"

"Negative. I mean I haven't turned up Mr. Nichols. His car is gone, so I assume he went somewhere in it. I've had an APB out on him around here and in neighboring New York State and Massachusetts. No dice."

"The heat's on," Quist said. "He's got to be found and protected."

"We're doing our best, Mr. Quist."

Quist called the Beaumont and asked for Lee Smith. Lydia didn't sound sleepy at all. He had to tell her about Walberg and the Hales and give her a sketch of their visit with Laverick.

"Where are you, Julian?"

"Home."

"I'm coming."

"No! Stay where you are, Lydia. You're safe there. Dan's with me and there are cops standing guard outside. I've got to get some sleep. I'm dead on my feet. I'll call you when I wake up."

At last he crawled out of his clothes and into the king-sized bed in his room. Garvey stayed on the couch in the living room with Quist's gun on the table beside him.

Quist fell into a deep druglike sleep.

He had to be dragged out of it. Garvey was shaking his shoulder, not gently. He opened his eyes and was blinded by sunshine. He glanced at his wristwatch, trying to remember why he was without Lydia. Eleven o'clock in the morning! He had slept almost a full eight hours.

"It's Connie," Dan said. He looked bright and hard. "Robson's our man." He gestured to the bedside phone. "Connie's still on the line."

Quist reached for it.

"I was full of jokes about what it cost me to play detective for you," Connie said. "Then Dan gave me the whole story of last night, boss. My God!"

"If you're sure about Max Robson, there may be a chance to help David," Quist said.

"I'm sure, boss. Robson turns in the copy on Sunday for his Tuesday column. I was there when my friend checked in this morning. We compared it with the letter you gave me —the-long-and-short-of-it one. No question it's the same typewriter. There are three or four letters slightly out of line. The same in both. He writes his column at home, by the way, which is in the Omaha Apartments on Central Park West."

"Thanks, doll. I hope the price wasn't too high."

"Rather fun, as a matter of fact," Connie said. "Be careful, boss."

"My middle name," Quist said. He put down the phone.

"We let Kreevich know?" Garvey asked.

"Let me think while I shower and shave," Quist said. "I have a feeling the cops may not be the way to break Robson."

"You're playing with David's life," Garvey said.

"I know—and Nichols's and mine."

He shaved and showered and felt a hundred percent revived, angry, impatient. Robson, a cheap gossip-mongering phony! Robson had set all this in motion with his threatening letters. For what purpose? Just the excitement of it, or was the aim blackmail? Or had he simply been out to harm David without any awareness of what was in the can of peas he'd opened?

Garvey had hot coffee on the bar when he got downstairs.

"I think I'd like for us to try Robson by ourselves," Quist said. "Kreevich will have to inform him of his rights. The sonofabitch has no rights as far as I'm concerned."

"He's a night person," Garvey said. "Chances are he'd still be home at this time of day."

"If Laverick hasn't found him faster than we have," Quist said.

The Omaha is an old Victorian hulk of a building that has housed a great many famous people in its day, and infamous ones, too, like Robson. Quist and Garvey hadn't been able to evade Kreevich's cops outside the Beekman Place building, and they accepted a ride in the patrol car to the Omaha. Quist called Robson on the house phone in the lobby. Robson answered promptly.

"It's Julian Quist. I'm down in the lobby."

Robson sounded relieved. "This is a little early in my day for social calls," he said.

"I want to talk to you about your typewriter," Quist said.

"My typewriter?"

"The one you wrote those letters to me on," Quist said.

"You're full of it!" Robson said. "I don't know what you're talking about."

"I have two choices if you don't invite me up," Quist said. "I can let the police know about you, or I can really let you have what you deserve and turn you over to Gerald Laverick."

"Jesus!" It was a long whisper. Then, after a moment: "Come up. It's Eight B."

The elevator was an old, grillwork iron cage. The hallway

was high ceilinged and dark, the door to 8 B heavy oak. Robson opened the door the instant Quist touched the bell. He looked like a sick man, shriveled inside his skin. Long afterwards Quist couldn't remember anything about the living room except that it was dark, expensively furnished, with what looked like old family portraits on the walls. Robson didn't seem to be able to speak. His mouth was twitching under the Fu Manchu mustache.

"I don't want to waste time with denials and protestations," Quist said in a cold voice. "You undoubtedly know that during the night Janice Trail and George Walberg were murdered. You may know that somebody tried to gun me down. You may know that the Hales are missing and may be dead. Now, we have compared the copy you delivered to the syndicate yesterday with the letters we've been receiving. Same typewriter. Don't say no, and don't say somebody else must have used it. I haven't the patience for that. Try it, and I'll pick up the phone and let Gerald Laverick decide what to do with you."

"I—I think I need a drink," Robson said.

"Make it a good one. It may be your last one on this earth if you don't come clean," Garvey said cheerfully.

Robson went somewhere into the dark recesses of the room and came back with a glass in a shaking hand.

"I swear to you, I never dreamed that anything like this would happen," Robson said.

"That you would be caught, or that you'd be responsible for several murders?" Quist said.

Robson sank down into the corner of a deep couch and swallowed thirstily. "It's not a short story," he said. Then his eyes rolled up. "Oh, God, I didn't mean that as a pun."

"The long and the short of it, you said in your first note to me."

"That was a double pun," Robson said. "I—I have to

begin at the beginning."

"Begin," Quist said. "And remember that more lives are at stake."

"My real name is Anthony Maxwell," Robson said. "My father was Jerry Maxwell, a foreign correspondent who also did some undercover intelligence work for the State Department. He was killed in an automobile accident when I was eight years old. That was thirty years ago this summer."

Another dead man in this crazy-quilt pattern, Quist thought.

"My mother and father and I were spending the summer in Geneva, Switzerland. All around us Europe was at war. I don't know what my father was involved with at the time, but he left us at the little inn where we were staying for a couple of days. He never came back. We got the word that his car had gone over a cliff into a bottomless lake. There was someone with him named Kurt Lang. My mother didn't know who Lang was except that my father had known him before the war. The newspapers said he was someone connected with a big chemical combine. Lang's body was never recovered. They assumed it had been thrown clear of the car which was surfaced. There was never any question raised about the accident."

"Should there have been?"

"I know now that my father was murdered by Kurt Lang and the car pushed over the cliff with my father's body in it. Lang simply disappeared—for a while."

Something about the way he talked made Quist think that telling this story was an enormous relief for Robson.

"My mother and I came back to this country," Robson said. "Things were very rough for us. We'd always lived well, but my father had evidently spent his money as fast as he made it. We were dead broke. My mother had no kind of training to prepare her for any kind of job. She waited on table, for God sake, in a Childs restaurant, and we lived in a cold-water flat.

"This had been going on for about three years. I was going to public school here in the city. That was when Robert Short came into our lives. I think he spoke to my mother in the restaurant where she was working, asked her for a date. Something like that. She was lonely. Anyhow, they struck up a friendship. He was teaching in a private school somewhere. He was a kind man, a generous man, but troubled. Something about his past that he never told us. Finally he asked my mother to marry him. I was delighted. It meant a better standard of living for us. I liked Robert Short. I liked him a lot."

"We don't have time to cover thirty years of your life," Garvey said.

"This part you have to know," Robson said. His forehead was beaded with sweat. "Rob Short became my stepfather. For two years we lived a comfortable, contented life. My mother and Short were not passionately in love, but he was considerate and kind, and her loneliness was cared for. Then one night when I was about thirteen Short came home in a highly disturbed state. He talked in private to my mother, and I know now he told her that something in his past had caught up with him and he was going to have to go into hiding for a while. We were to change our names, deny any knowledge of him. He left us that night and I never saw him again.

"The next we heard of him was that he had been arrested on a morals charge in a small Vermont town. There was one word from him, a letter to my mother. Don't come to his aid. Don't make any effort to help him. If we were approached, deny that we had ever heard of him or it might cost us our lives. It sounded very melodramatic, but somehow we believed him." Robson emptied his glass and looked hungrily toward the dark corner of the room. "The next we heard he had hung himself in jail." He stood up and walked unsteadily toward the source of supply. He came back with his glass filled. "That's all that matters about Robert Short until about four months ago."

"A gap of twenty-five years," Quist said.

"A part of my life that is of no interest to anyone—except some odds and ends. My name. Max, from my father's name, Maxwell. And a rather silly conceit, my last name—Rob's son, after my stepfather. Then came a letter, a long, typewritten letter. Unsigned, postmarked here in the city. It wasn't believable, yet I read it over and over. The writer identified me as Jerry Maxwell's son and Robert Short's stepson. My father, he told me, had not died in an accident. He had been murdered by Kurt Lang, the man who had apparently died with him. My father, the letter writer said, had been about to expose a huge criminal conspiracy by a great corporate empire—Laverick Enterprises. Laverick had been dealing with the enemy—a traitor, a betrayer. Kurt Lang was Laverick's agent, the letter said. Lang, having betrayed my father and killed him, had turned soft and had tried to make up for his treachery and his crime. How? By coming into our lives as Robert Short and taking care of my mother and me." Robson took a swallow of his drink, and then he laughed, a jangled sound. "Do you speak German, Quist?"

"No."

"The German word for 'long' is 'lang.' My little joke to you, Quist, my little clue. 'The long and the short of it.' Short and Lang were the same man—the man in the snapshot."

"Why send to me?" Quist asked.

"You'll see," Robson said. "The letter went on. To reveal what I was being told would simply mean I'd be wiped out by Laverick. But there might be a way to get money from him—large sums of money for me and the letter writer—in return for silence. But my identity must be carefully hidden or I was a dead man. I must destroy the letter, for if it fell into anyone's hands I was done for."

"Did you ask your mother about this story?" Quist asked.

The corner of Robson's mouth twitched. "My mother died ten years ago of cancer." He sighed. "I thought the whole thing was a crackpot piece of nonsense. But I destroyed the letter."

"Were there instructions on how to contact the writer?" Garvey asked.

"No. But soon there was another letter. In it was a clipping about a hunting accident in Dabney, Vermont. Two men named Williams—one of them had been the boy involved in the Short scandal, the other his father, a famous lawyer. The letter said that Luther Williams, the lawyer, had stumbled onto the truth about Lang and Short and my real father's murder. He had tried to blackmail Laverick. This would demonstrate to me how clever we would have to be if we were to try to put the squeeze on Laverick. It pointed out that I could get revenge for my father and become rich and independent if I played my cards right. Well, I decided to do a little sniffing around myself. I ski. So I shifted my skiing activities to Dabney, Vermont."

"Skytop Lodge," Quist said.

"You have done your homework," Robson said bitterly. "I burned that second letter, too, by the way. I found out nothing in Dabney. The hunting accident seemed to have been just that, a hunting accident. I couldn't talk to the lawyer who had defended my stepfather. He was a hopeless stroke victim. I drew a blank there, although I went back for several weekends."

"But you did find someone who would mail me a letter, addressed to the Dabney House, on Saturday morning."

Robson looked up, his eyes puzzled. "I never wrote you

a letter at the Dabney House, Saturday or any other time."

"I got it."

"If you still have it, you'll find it wasn't written on my typewriter."

So much for that, Quist thought. He'd heard men lie and he was curiously certain that the frightened Robson was telling the truth.

"About a week ago I got a small package in the mail," Robson said. "It contained a couple of dozen copies of the snapshot I sent you of Short and the Williams boy. There was also a letter that outlined a plan of action. We would use David Hale as a fall guy. I liked that part of it. I hate the bastard. The purpose was to get you, or the network, or the advertising agency, or Hale himself to start digging for the truth. Whoever undertook the investigation we would feed with clues. And we would keep warning Laverick that unless he paid we would lead the investigator to solid evidence that would blow the whole story wide open. A major part of Laverick's empire would crumble, and he'd probably be tried for treason. So I decided to play along." Robson drew a deep breath. "We sent letters to all of you, and you were the one, Quist, who took the bait. So I followed up on you."

"And there were also follow-ups to Laverick?"

"Yes. Of course he recognized the snapshot and he knew we had something."

"But you didn't have anything, except letters from an unknown," Garvey said.

"You don't doubt today, do you, that whoever it is had run down the story to the last detail?" Robson asked.

"No."

Robson twisted his body as though he was in pain. "I should have known there was no way to beat Laverick. But I never dreamed he would set out calmly to kill everyone who might have the smallest lead."

"So we tell your story," Garvey said.

"Without any evidence? Without even the letters that got me started? Without knowing who the hell it is who does know the truth?" Robson cried out. "And you'll be committing murder, because Laverick will come after me. Right now he has no idea I'm involved."

"You haven't got a clue as to who your letter writer is?"

"No." Robson laughed, a hysterical-sounding laugh. "Would you believe, when it was suggested David Hale should be the fall guy, I thought it might be Janice Trail? She hated him so much. He might have talked to her at some time about the Short case. He lived with her intimately for two years. So I gave her a copy of the snapshot the other night at the party. I was riding high, getting careless. I thought she might react. She didn't. Somebody danced off with her and later, when I asked her for the snapshot back, she found she'd lost it. She'd had it in her evening bag, guessed it must have fallen out when she was using the bag in the powder room. But Laverick took her anyway."

Quist was thinking of Abbie Tyler, poor, innocent, starstruck kid. She'd probably picked up the snapshot in the powder room, kept it as a souvenir of her contact with the great movie queen.

"What are you going to do?" Robson asked. "Are you going to point at me? Are you going to let Laverick kill me? For God's sake, Quist!"

"Without proof to back up his story, we just set him up as a target," Garvey said to Quist.

Quist was silent for a long time. "I think," he said finally, "there is a way to make Laverick show his hand. The risk will be mine and not yours, Robson. But if I survive it, you're going to need a very good lawyer to defend you against charges of blackmail and extortion and withholding evidence that could have prevented murder."

FOUR

By early afternoon millions of people had heard the news. Janice Trail had been murdered. David Hale and his wife had been kidnaped and his personal secretary murdered. The police connected the two tragedies. Julian Quist, Hale's public relations man had been shot at on the street by a would-be assassin. Enough gore to satisfy the bloodthirstiest. And there was more. That night at eleven-thirty, if David Hale had not been released, Julian Quist would go on Night Talk in his place and make an appeal to the kidnapers.

In Quist's apartment there were violent protests to the scheme. Garvey was stubbornly against it. Kreevich listened and wondered and argued that the risk was too great. Lydia, hearing the news on the television set in her hotel room at the Beaumont, had broken her solemn promise to Quist and come flying to Beekman Place.

In the offices of Julian Quist Associates, high above Grand Central Station, Connie Parmalee, her face a pale mask, was heading a staff of researchers to find a fact. Somewhere there must be a record of some corporate deal, some power combine, that would expose Laverick's dealing with the enemy in the early days of World War II, the story Jerry Maxwell was about to reveal when Laverick's man Lang—or Short—betrayed him and killed him. Not much hope in the time they had, but they would keep trying till the last minute. Till eleven-thirty, when Quist, Connie guessed, would step out into the open and turn himself into a sitting duck.

Quist's plan was not complicated. Night Talk was staged in a Broadway theater. Quist would go before the cameras in David's place. There would be a telephone beside him on the stage with a special number. He would threaten to reveal a story he knew that would disclose the identity of the mastermind behind the crimes unless the kidnapers phoned the special number and made the necessary arrangements to release the Hales unharmed. They would break for a commercial—a sales talk for, ironically, Laverick Enterprises. If there had been no call, he would begin to tell the story of Jerry Maxwell's murder and the man named Kurt Lang, who had betrayed him and done him in. Another commercial break. Then, if there had been no call, he would begin to go into detail; Lang was not dead, had reappeared under the name of Short. He would let the story out, inch by inch, hoping that Laverick would deal for the Hales before Quist finally named him.

"Why should he deal?" Garvey argued. "He has to know you don't have evidence, because if you had you would have gone to the police with it, and the FBI and the CIA, and, for God sake, the President, instead of staging this little drama."

"Because if the story is accurate, he'll know I got it from someone who does have evidence," Quist said.

"Unless Robson was bullshitting us," Garvey said.

"I don't think so."

"So Laverick does one of two things," Garvey said. "You're doing the show in a theater. There's a live audience. Someone in the audience shoots you down while you sit there on the stage. Someone sneaks into the wings of the theater."

"He'll let it go a long way," Quist said, "in the hope I'll let some clue slip as to the source of my information. Either he'll deal for the Hales or he'll let it go to the very end."

"It's comforting to know you'll have ninety minutes to live after you go on the air," Lydia said in a very small voice.

"Oh, he may wait beyond that, Lydia," Garvey said. "He may wait to sue for libel, take everything Julian has or will ever have, and get him later. This man is a psychotic freak. A traitor, a betrayer. You named him in his own office, Julian, without knowing it. A Judas freak!"

"What else can we do?" Quist asked his friends. "Nothing, while there's still a chance for the Hales?"

And so it went, round and round, until, surprisingly, Kreevich went along with Quist. The police could cover the audience quite openly. The backstage could be thoroughly guarded. He suggested that he himself go on camera before Quist, inform the audience that Quist was in danger and that the police scattered in the house were prepared to pounce on anyone who made the slightest overt move. If Laverick's people knew they didn't have a chance, it might persuade them to deal for the Hales.

"And after they turn David and Peggy loose, won't they still have to go after Julian?" Lydia asked in a small voice.

"They have to keep after all of us, luv, until we find the man who has the proof," Quist said.

"Why doesn't he come forward?"

"Because he still hopes to squeeze a fortune out of Laverick," Garvey said. "When we're all dead, Laverick will find he's still getting letters!"

The argument was over. The day wore into evening. Quist and Lydia found themselves strangely withdrawn. He loved her, she thought, and yet he was perfectly willing to commit suicide. She felt unimportant, unwanted, deserted. He, on his part, loved her so much, wanted her so much, he was afraid if he gave way to it his own determination might break down. So they spoke politely and stayed apart.

In the early evening an exhausted Connie reported. No evidence but some guesswork.

"Before the war Laverick bought Schwartzkopf Chemical, a German company," she told Quist. "He never divested himself of that ownership. He owns it now. It's only a guess, but it could be that Jerry Maxwell discovered that American money, Laverick's money, was keeping Schwartzkopf going during the war, supplying the Nazis with chemicals and plastics vital to their war effort. It's only a guess, boss, but if it's true it could destroy Laverick even at this late date."

"It sounds like a hell of a good guess," Quist said.

"Boss?"

"Yes?"

"Don't do it!"

"I don't think I have any choice, doll," Quist said gently.

And then, a little later, after a supper that nobody ate, there was a call from Trooper Spofford in Dabney. Esther Moffet had lost her battle for life. There was no sign or word from Walter Nichols. His car hadn't been spotted. No accident, no news of any sort.

At ten o'clock Quist went upstairs to dress for the evening —a rust brown dinner jacket speckled with threads as gold as his hair. He hoped that Lydia would come up, but she stayed downstairs with Garvey and Kreevich. When he was ready to join them he wrote a note and left it on the pillow on her side of the king-sized bed. It wasn't a witty note. It said simply, "I love you totally."

Night Talk was staged in the old Havemeyer Theater on Broadway in the Fifties. The Havemeyer had been transformed some years ago into a television studio for live audience productions. The main changes in the building from the days when it used to house Broadway musicals were the glassed-in control booth suspended from the first balcony and the glassed-in client's booth off to one side at the same level. There were four cameras placed at different angles to the stage. In the control booth there were four monitors, and the director and assistant director could see four pictures on those monitors and choose the one that could go out to the public, from close-ups to side views to panoramas of the whole stage. The client's booth was reserved for the sponsor, or for special guests, shutting these favored people away from the public audience.

When Quist and his party arrived at the Havemeyer, long lines of people were waiting hopefully to get in. Quist, Lydia, Garvey, and their police escort went to the stage-door entrance and into the theater, where an anxious director and crew waited. The stage was set with futuristic-looking drapes and flats, but was bare of furnishing except for four comfortable armchairs with a sort of coffee table set in front of them. On the table was a water pitcher, four glasses, ashtrays, and, on this night, a telephone.

The director explained that there was no bell on the telephone. A large red light would go on if anyone called in to the special number—824–7285.

"We thought something visual would make more sense than the sound of a bell," the director said. "You're going to be alone on stage?"

"Yes," Quist said.

"I wanted to get an early shot of the house itself," the director said. "There are twenty uniformed policemen stationed along the side aisles and at the back of the house. More in the balcony."

Kreevich wasn't taking chances. Backstage, in the dark corridors and dressing room areas, were more cops, uniformed and in plain clothes.

"I think I'd like it if Lydia were to watch this from the client's booth," Quist said. "Safest place in the house except the control booth. Will you take her there, Dan?"

Garvey nodded. Lydia didn't look at Quist. He reached

out to touch her but she had already started to move away with Garvey. Quist settled the final details with the director. Kreevich would appear first and make his announcement, and then Quist would take the stage and begin his bargaining for life or death.

"There's a makeup man waiting for you in the offstage dressing room," the director said.

Quist hesitated. "I think I'd rather play it as I am," he said. "I may not be as pretty that way, but with all that muck on my face I don't think I'd feel quite real."

The director glanced at his watch. "I'd better get up to the control booth," he said. "We have just under ten minutes to go. Good luck."

"Pray for it," Quist said.

Garvey and Kreevich came back on stage together. They were all hidden from the buzzing audience by the drawn curtain.

"Who do you think's in the client's booth?" Garvey said. "Laverick, his secretary Miss Atwater, Jason Crown, and Joe Malik. I'm not sure that's the place for Lydia, but Kreevich . . ."

"I have a cop standing behind each one of them," Kreevich said. "I explained politely that anyone connected with David Hale might be in danger. The Great Man expressed himself as grateful for my concern. But Lydia's safe there, and she might see something or hear something."

"All the cops in the world can't stop Laverick from giving a prearranged signal when he decides I've talked too much," Quist said. "All it tells us is that the attack won't come from the client's booth."

"Would you believe that no one else of importance has risked coming?" Garvey said. "The network people, the agency people, all decided they'd rather watch it at home. Of course, if there is anything they can do for you, Julian—The bastards!"

"Two minutes to go," a stage manager said. "If you'll step offstage, gentlemen, we'll open the curtain."

They moved out into the wings.

"Where are you going to be, Dan?" Quist asked. His mouth felt dry.

"Right here," Garvey said, "as close to you as I can be without being seen." He reached out and closed a strong hand over Quist's arm. "You can still give it up, Julian, even now."

"I think I have to go through with it, Dan."

"Luck!"

The stage manager pointed a finger at Kreevich and said, "Go!" They were on the air with millions of people watching.

Kreevich walked out onto the apron of the stage and held up his hands for silence.

"I am Lieutenant Kreevich, Homicide, New York Police Department," he said. "As most of you know, we are in the midst of a rash of killings and the kidnaping of David Hale and his wife. It is our hope that through the medium of this telecast we can contact the kidnapers and make some sort of deal for David Hale's release. Mr. Julian Quist will try to make that contact. Mr. Quist knows almost all there is to know about this case and he will try to be persuasive. But he is in danger when he steps out onto this stage. That's why there are so many policemen in the audience. I want to warn you that if there is any kind of disturbance or outcry here in the theater, my men will act first and ask questions afterwards. Thank you."

Kreevich exited and Quist walked out onto the stage. The applause was thunderous. He went over and sat down in one of the chairs next to the telephone and waited for silence. He looked up toward the client's booth, but the bright television lights made it impossible for him to see behind the glass panel where Lydia watched with Laverick and his party.

Finally there was silence, and Quist leaned forward and spoke in a low, earnest voice. "Ladies and gentlemen, here in the theater and in millions of homes across the country. There is a saying to the effect that the past determines our future. As the lieutenant pointed out to you we have had a bloody weekend, a slaughter of innocent people, and the abduction of the man who should be here tonight instead of me. It's my hope that he and his wife can be saved. It's my intention to try to bargain for them here and now. What I have to offer is silence in return for David Hale and his wife. What do I have to be silent about? This is what I have to make clear to them. I will begin by hinting at the truth in the hope that the hints will convince them that my silence will be invaluable to them. You see this telephone on the table, ladies and gentlemen? It has a special number. That number is 824–7285. I repeat, 824–7285. While I am talking, and during the commercial breaks, if the kidnapers will contact me, perhaps we can make a deal. I urge people who wish me well, or who have advice, not to call this number. Please leave it open for the kidnapers. And now this, directly to the kidnapers. I will hint at first at what I know. But before this hour and a half of air time is over, if I haven't heard from you at this special number, I will spell out the complete story in detail—crimes, places, names.

"And now to begin." Quist's handsome face was set in hard angular lines. "The past determines our future. This bloody weekend was forecast by an event that took place thirty years ago. Two men were driving in an automobile somewhere in the Swiss Alps. Their car apparently went out of control, plunged down a rocky cliff and into the icy waters of a Swiss lake. One body was found in the wreckage of the car, the other was never recovered, presumably drawn by currents, out of reach, to the bottom of the lake. No one ever questioned that it had been an accident until some ten years later. Then, two men were deer hunting in the Vermont hills and they were both shot down in what was accepted as a hunting accident. But I tell you that was no more an accident than that first incident in the Swiss Alps. In that first case the man who was not found was never lost. He had killed the other man and propelled the car with his victim in it over the cliff. It was murder, and the murderer walked away, changed his name and identity, and wasn't suspected until ten years later. The two deer hunters had stumbled on the truth, and they were murdered to keep them silent. By the same man? No, because that man was long dead, a suicide. But the man who planned both the so-called accidents was the same, a man who hires killers, a man who is responsible for the horrors of this weekend. I ask him now, is that enough to convince you that you should deal with me for the Hales? I suggest you call 824–7285 during the following commercial."

Quist leaned back in his chair and from the control booth a taped commercial about one of Laverick's industries appeared on the monitors and the home screens.

From the wings Garvey was gesturing frantically to Quist. Quist hesitated, and then got up and walked into the wings. If the red light showed on the phone, the audience would react enough to get him back on stage.

"Friend of yours," Garvey said.

And there was Walter Nichols, Old Nick, looking bedraggled and worn.

"Nick, where the hell have you been?" Quist asked.

"Around," the old man said in a dull voice. "You know that Esther's dead."

"Yes, I'm sorry."

"I heard what you were up to and I got down here as fast as I could. You think it will work?"

Quist had turned his head so that he could see the phone. No red light. "It looks as if we'll have to give them a little more," he said. "But it's not safe for you to be wandering around, Nick. Dan, take him up to the client's booth. Lydia's there, Nick, and she can bring you up-to-date."

The stage manager was signaling frantically to Quist to get back on camera. He gave the old man a pat on the shoulder and went out again into the cruel white lights.

"Unfortunately," he said to the audience, "my preliminary remarks have not brought us a phone call. Let me ask you in the audience a question. If you knew that a man, an American man, was providing an enemy with money and material to help kill our soldiers in a war, would you grant him amnesty thirty years later?"

There was a rumble of protest from the audience in the theater.

"I tell you and the kidnapers of David Hale that it was to hide that fact that an accident was staged in the Swiss Alps and that two men were shot to death while deer hunting in Vermont. And I tell you that nineteen years after that deer hunting accident we have had this bloody weekend to keep that fact hidden. Why would a man betray his country, you ask? The answer is for profit. Whole segments of our society have long believed that profits are more important than patriotism or people. And now, if what I have said doesn't turn the light red on that telephone, I will begin to spell it out. But before I do—"

Quist got no further. There was the unmistakable sound of a fusillade of gunshots from somewhere in the audience. Women in the balcony began to scream. Instinctively Quist ducked out of his chair and headed for the wings. He was instantly surrounded by cops, who had no idea what was going on in the house.

And then Garvey came running, his face ashen. "Your old friend from Vermont," he said.

Quist felt sick. "They got him?"

"Not exactly," Garvey said. He moistened his lips. "Like you said, I got him to Lydia in the client's booth. He took one look at Laverick and then shouted at the top of his lungs: 'Like the man says, no amnesty, Laverick!' Then he took a gun out of his pocket and shot Laverick three times in the head before one of the cops gunned him down."

There was only the dim light of a bedside lamp in the hospital room. The old man on the bed was very near to death. His breath made a rattling sound in his throat.

"He killed Esther," he whispered.

Quist sat beside him, holding a cold hand in his. "You were the man who started all this, weren't you, Nick? You were the man who wrote to Max Robson and gave him the facts."

"Greatest newspaper story of this century. I spent better than twenty years trying to dig up the evidence. But I didn't have the nerve to print it," the old man whispered. "Laverick was too powerful. I liked living. But—but I thought I could put the heat on him, make him pay. I—I never dreamed he'd try to solve his problem by wiping out everybody in sight. Poor little Abbie! Poor Esther! Oh, Jesus, Julian!" He coughed, and there was blood on the tissue he held to his mouth. "But I stopped him, Julian. I stopped him, didn't I?"

"You stopped him, Nick. Where is the evidence, the proof?"

"Spent all day making it up into a package for you. Mailed it to your office in case I didn't see you. But I saw you, didn't I, Julian? I saw you." He coughed again. "You're a good man, Julian, a brave man." He gave Quist a terrible imitation of a grin. "Loose ends department. I mailed you that letter in Dabney Saturday morning. I knew you'd come."

"I had it figured," Quist said, "while I was waiting to be let in here."

"David? Is there any chance for him and his wife?"

"They're safe," Quist said. "The lawyer, Jason Crown, cracked. The strong-arm boys have taken to the woods."

"No more profit in it," Old Nick said. "You were right, Julian. I started it all for profit. I was going to retire rich. I cared more about profit than people." He seemed to strangle, pushed himself up on his elbow, gasping for breath. And then he came to the end of his road.

Lydia and Garvey and Kreevich were having a sort of breakfast on the terrace at Quist's apartment. The sun was just beginning to rise, deep red in the East. They were waiting for Quist to come back from the hospital from what they knew would be a death watch.

Words and facts had spewed out of Jason Crown like a flood from a broken water main. The Hales, held in an apartment in Queens, had been watching the television when the whole story broke from the Havemeyer. The masked men who had held them had run out and left them free when the news came that Gerald Laverick was dead. They had been questioned for hours to the point of exhaustion. Evidently Laverick thought they might have some physical evidence, some proof of Robert Short's real identity. Without that there was no case against him. Anyone who had known Short might have such proof, including Miss Moffet and Sam Hamner. When he couldn't find what he wanted Laverick turned to total destruction of everyone in any way connected.

"Small point that's been sticking in my craw," Garvey said. "A World War Two German Luger pistol."

"It belonged to Laverick," Kreevich said.

"You're kidding. He shot Abbie?"

"No, no. But he carried it in the glove compartment of his car. Liked it better than a modern piece. That night of David's party, when everybody got letters, Laverick got the notion that David might be his blackmailer. He left the Beaumont early with Malik and sent Malik to search David's apartment for that proof of Short's identity. Malik took the old man's car, and before he broke into the apartment, he checked his own gun. There was something wrong with it. So he borrowed the Luger in the glove compartment. When the girl caught him, he shot her, and it sounded to him like a cannon. So he got out of there without completing his search."

There was the sound of a key in the front door, and Quist came out onto the terrace. He looked done in.

"It's finished," he said. He told them Nick's story.

Kreevich got up from his chair. "Not quite," he said. "We've got Malik, but there's the rest of Laverick's army to find. Crown will be useful, I hope. Tomorrow, the next day, I'll need your help in putting it all together, Julian, if there is a package of evidence.

"Sure. There'll be a package. Nick had no reason to lie."

The lieutenant leered at Garvey. "Can I drop you off on my way downtown?"

"Oh! Yeah, fine," Garvey said.

"Thanks, Dan," Quist said.

"Like the fellow said, it was nothing."

"You stood by, chum. That's everything."

Garvey and Kreevich left.

"A double bourbon on the rocks?" Lydia asked.

Quist nodded and sank down in one of the wicker chairs. She came back in a moment with his drink, and he took some of it gratefully.

"I see by that housecoat that you've been upstairs," he

said. "Did you find my note?"

"Yes."

"I'd like to explain—"

"There's nothing to explain, my darling," she said. "It was —well, just that I was so damned scared for you. You need rest. Would you like to sleep alone?"

He smiled at her. "You have to be kidding," he said.